Tokens of Grace

Tokens of Grace

A Novel in Stories

Sheila O'Connor

Drawings by Sharon Brown

MILKWEED EDITIONS

TOKENS OF GRACE

© 1990, *text by Sheila O'Connor*
© 1990, *drawings by Sharon Brown*

Printed in the United States of America
Published in 1990 by *Milkweed Editions*
Post Office Box 3226
Minneapolis, Minnesota 55403
Books may be ordered from the above address

93 92 91 90   4 3 2 1

ISBN: 0-915943-47-6

"FLOWERS ON THE WALL"
  (Lew Dewitt)
© 1966 UNICHAPPEL MUSIC, INC.
All Rights Reserved. Used By Permission.

"DAISY BELL"
© 1892 T.B. Harms and Co.

Publication of this book is made possible in part by grant support from
the Literature Program of the National Endowment for the Arts, the
Arts Development Fund of United Arts, the Dayton Hudson Foundation for Dayton's and Target Stores, the First Bank System Foundation,
the General Mills Foundation, the Jerome Foundation, the Minnesota
State Arts Board through an appropriation by the Minnesota State
Legislature, a McKnight Foundation Award administered by the Minnesota State Arts Board, the Northwest Area Foundation, and by the
support of generous individuals.

Library of Congress Cataloging-in-Publication Data

O'Connor, Sheila.
    Tokens of grace / by Sheila O'Connor.
      p.   cm.
    ISBN 0-915943-47-6
    I. Title.
  PS3565.C645T64   1990
  813'.54—dc20   90-5438
                                                          CIP

For Elizabeth,
with love and gratitude.

For my family,
here and gone.

By Heart

Desire

Surviving

Witness

Finished

Mercy

Parts of this book appeared in slightly altered form in *Helicon Nine*, Number 20, 1989.

The author would like to thank The Loft for a 1989 Loft/McKnight Award which made it possible for her to complete this book.

Special thanks to Marty Case, John Caddy, and Callie Cardamon for their generous attention to the manuscript, and to Tricia O'Connor for her advice and assistance.

". . . You know the mind, how it comes on the scene again
and makes tiny histories of things, and the imagination
how it wants everything back one more time . . . "

Richard Hugo, *"Letter to Matthews
from Barton Street Flats"*

By Heart

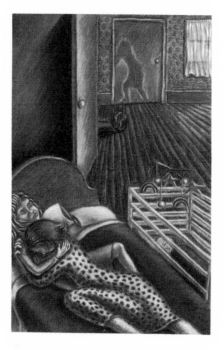

THE ASSASSINATION

The assassination happens in their sleep. In the murky light of Callie and Ryan's bedroom, they open their eyes to their mother's face hovering above their beds. Other nights have been the same. A desperate voice dragging them from dreams. Hurry up. We're leaving. Baby Tessa's head smothered in blankets so their father doesn't hear his family disappear. Their car rolling down the driveway before the key is turned. The nights of streets, her sisters huddled in the back seat, Callie up front, trying to talk their mother into going home. The old, frantic question — What would you do if you were me? Off the highway there is always a morning, and they go back to Frosted Flakes and the sun washing across the knife nicks on the breakfast table. Their father, stretched out face up, snores on the living room floor. Callie and Ryan deal out hands of Go to the Dump on his stomach.

In the daylight, the nights are a secret they keep, a lie that belongs in a story. But tonight their mother does not take them from their beds; instead she covers her eyes with her robe and repeats, They have shot Bobby Kennedy. They have shot Bobby Kennedy.

Callie pulls her mother into bed, smells the night skin of salt and summer. Not again, not again, her mother cries, burying her sharp wet nose in Callie's neck. A small breath rises from Tessa's crib.

Quiet, Callie says. You'll wake the baby.

Who is Bobby Kennedy? Callie remembers the other Kennedy killing and how the cartoons were cancelled for days because of the funeral. At kindergarten they recited the Pledge of Allegiance over and over, and Mrs. Weebush said they were living their own history. They cut out pictures from magazines, Caroline and John John next to the flag-draped casket and John John's brave salute. That salute made the whole country sorry. In Callie's baby book there is a newspaper clipping of Jackie Kennedy expecting. But who is Bobby Kennedy and why was he shot in the middle of sleep, and does he have his own family? Into the sheets her mother mumbles clues about a woman in a polka-dot dress, the woman is a piece of the mystery.

Tonight Callie feels scared for Bobby, but she is glad they won't have to leave. Asleep, she dreams of her mother's hair, combed into a high, ratty beehive, and a polka-dot dress that follows the bones of her mother's body. A black revolver shakes in her mother's hand. There is a slam like a closed door, and her father falls without speaking. Callie opens her eyes to her own whispered *Daddy*. Her mother's leg drapes across Callie's leg, hot and heavy. And Callie, pinned by the weight, understands that somewhere on a kitchen floor one man's story is ending.

RYAN

Lamb of God who takes away the sins of the world, Ryan repeats every word, her memory exact.

That's really something, he says, shaking his head. You've got the whole damn Mass down straight.

Outside Our Lady of the Lake, Callie and Ryan sit with him on the steps. Too crowded, he says every Sunday once the spring sets in. Too crowded and too stuffy. Callie rests her cheek on the furry surface of his knee, traces the frayed threads along the hem of his Bermuda shorts.

God is everywhere, Ryan knows, so the church isn't necessary. God can see us inside and out, Ryan says, hopscotching down the crumbling church steps. God sees everything.

Cars drive by slowly; slowly is Sunday.

Act like a lady, he tells Ryan, when he and Callie go in for Communion. I expect you to behave.

Communion comes after *Lord I am not worthy*. Ryan knows the lines, but their meaning stays a mystery. *Worthy* is a word she hasn't learned. With a gift for memory, at school Ryan recites the prayers by heart. By heart, her mother calls it, which means it lives inside you permanently.

Ryan unbuckles her black patent leathers, offers them to the sun. Shine in the night like God's eyes. And where are God's eyes? Everywhere. God, she says aloud, and God answers, I'm here. What's he sound like exactly? Callie always asks, her question a trick to prove Ryan is lying. Like Dad when he's singing. But Callie thinks she's imagining, imagining or just plain lying. But he does speak, and today, with the June breeze sliding between her open toes, she knows God is listening. Jitters jump in Ryan's stomach, the thrill of feeling the weather changing. Nervous tingling, like the night before a holiday, knowing that soon something huge is coming. The grass feels it, too, because it lifts its small stems to heaven.

Last ones out, Callie and her dad appear at the white wooden door. *Go in peace to love and serve the Lord.* All the way to the car, Callie's hands stay pressed in prayer. He taps the pack of cigarettes against his palm, flip-top box. Ryan tucks her anklets into her shiny shoes.

Hey, he says, shutting the door to the back seat. Try to keep those on your feet.

Every Sunday Callie rides up front to the Downbeat. After Mass there are lunches in the empty bar, cellophane bags of Happy Popcorn and Coke foaming from a long hose. Callie and Ryan spin the stools into a race, contest to see who whirls back first.

He gives quarters for the jukebox, shouts, Hey, punch *The Twist* for me. Then they join him in the frantic dance, hips wiggle, arms swing. Get down, girls, be a washing machine.

Sunday afternoon setup. Sticky beer glues their shoes to the dance floor. The Downbeat needs cleaning from the night before, and he waltzes the shaggy mop across the room. The silver ball of colored lights rotates over the Downbeat, paints Callie and Ryan into stars, stains lavender their round mouths ooohhhing into the microphones. Callie pretends to play the drums, Ryan strums an invisible guitar. Extra cash is Sundays, a way to make a buck stretch. The girls place a tin ashtray in the center of every table, make sure the chairs are pushed under all the way. Their reward is loose change, coins forgotten in the slot behind the jukebox, quarters that didn't take or songs that never played.

Now he wants to do the Limbo. Ryan grips one end of the mop handle. Callie backbends under, her body arched in a cloth rainbow.

Lower, lower, he shouts, until Callie's fingertips touch the floor. You should always try harder, he tells Callie afterward, knuckles kneading into Callie's head. You can always be better.

Come here, he says to Ryan, and the two girls settle against his stomach, breathe the smoke and beer of his body. Huge arms swallow them. Then they are pushed away, turned to look into his face, Listen to me.

Heads tilted, he lifts their chins with his hands. I want you to understand, this doesn't have anything to do with me. Hands back in his front pocket, he scrambles for a cigarette. You're old enough to face it.

Callie tugs his wrist, Come on Dad, let's dance again.

Honey, don't make this worse than it is.

But Callie is away from him and out the door, the daylight a shock in the dark of the Downbeat.

This is our day, Ryan tells him, and no one can take it away.

CALLIE

Callie crosses the orange traffic cones of caution. From the high seat of the bulldozer his dark face smiles down on her, black hair, dirt, skin thick and brown from the sun. He kills the motor, sets his hard hat aside, runs the front of his wrinkled T-shirt across the sweat on his forehead, climbs down. Wet lips and dust brush Callie's mouth. A Pall Mall appears, familiar lighter with the gold camel grinds under the force of his thumb.

Hold your head up, honey, he tells her when she hunches under the whistles of the other construction workers. What is it today, sweet baby?

There is nothing to say, but since she has discovered her father working on this street, she comes every day on her walk home from school. The first day he said she looked like a million bucks in her plaid jumper. Uniforms give you a sense that you're better. Now he looks long at her, waiting for an answer. He will make her say why she bothers him at work. But there is no reason, except that he no longer sleeps on the living room floor; she misses the sound of his songs while he shaves, and she feels like a part of her own body is lost. If she visits him on the street every day, maybe she can fill up the space he has left her. Talk to your mother, he tells her when she asks him to come back. She's the one calling the shots.

While the jackhammer rips into the concrete, Callie plans what to say next.

Get that kid out of here, a man carrying tubes of paper yells.

Sweetheart, he says, bending down to offer his back. We've got to move, it's too dangerous.

I'll walk, she tells him, too old for rides. Besides, I'm in my uniform. I don't want those men to see up my skirt.

You're growing up too fast for your old man to keep track. You're growing up without me.

Folded into a small square in her bookbag, a note waits. At recess Callie composed it, begging him to come home. Words she cannot say to his face, because even on the swingset, the sentences stuck in her throat. But Sister Ursula said Callie had a duty to let him know how much it hurt her. She said it was a girl's responsibility to get her own parents back together. Sister offered to check her words, but Callie is a good speller. *To My Dad Who Loves Me*, Callie wrote in red crayon. Hollow hearts with her initials decorate the edge. It was tough to get past that beginning, to outline the plan specifically, but Callie knows she can save her family. More nights she will watch Ryan and Tessa, so her parents can make a life. We have no life, is what her mother told her. And I'm tired of taking care of him. But Callie can take over.

Come home, she wrote. I will wash and fold your clothes. I can even cook you supper, if you let me. You said there wasn't anything in the world you wouldn't do for me.

But what if his promise ended with the marriage?

You're on the clock, the man yells again. Let's get this job done before the end of the day.

Okay, okay! Her dad waves him away. Sweetheart, for Christ's sake, you can't stop by here every day. You understand, don't you? I've got a job to do. What is it you want from me?

Callie cannot say. The note tells the truth, but the words don't come when she speaks. Maybe she can mail the note. But where is he living?

I've got to get going, he tells her. Take it easy. And

don't forget you've got your work cut out for you. You promised to take care of your sisters for me. Remember?

Yes, Callie says.

Honey, he says, I need to know. Are you with me?

MOTHER

She will sell the silver for the first month's rent, cash
in the useless collection of rose-handled utensils, ridiculous
reminder of her bridal shower and her mother's insistence
that nice wives found fine dinnerware a necessity. A legacy
of false propriety her daughters will do without. Now she
is no longer a wife, and the silver tarnishes in the dusty
mahogany box. She can sell it before the settlement —
money he won't know she owns — trade it in for the rent
on a basement apartment in Barren, a two-bedroom box
her children will call home. They are leaving him
behind — the violent requests to see his daughters, his 2
A.M. rantings. The silver will insure their escape, a new
home near her new job with the promise of a raise.

In 1957, her girlfriends gathered in her mother's living
room, nibbled soft mints and squares of cake. On the
sickening white frosting, blue raindrops drizzled down a
wedding bell umbrella. The girls told stories of sorority
pledges and handsome professors, passed around each gift
of silver. The guests swelled with the pride of their
generosity; even a pickle fork cost a small fortune. Their
fingers twitched toward their own collections, sunny
homes they'd decorate someday, successful husbands. They
said she was so lucky to skip college, the exams were such
a drag. Between gifts, she slipped away to the bathroom to
gag, her secret swallowed like sour spit.

On the organ her mother played *Daisy, Daisy, give me
your answer do*. Arms linked, the girls formed a chain,
swayed back and forth, sang. *It won't be a stylish marriage*.
Sweat trickled down between her heavy, tender breasts.
There were doorprize numbers written under paper plates,
shower games, dull discussions of home decorations,
recipes, her wedding dress.

23

I can't wait till it happens to me, they said, leaving. Then it was kisses at the door and Good luck, Joan, we'll see you on the big day.

Her mother pressed the carnation corsage for a souvenir, packed the silver in her hope chest. You'll thank me someday, she said. You got yourself into this mess; the least you can do is make it right by having a decent wedding. In her bedroom, James Dean's dreamy eyes blessed her and Callie, curled up in her belly like a question mark.

She had gotten married properly, but that didn't make the marriage happy. Her bridal shower belonged to another decade, an age of teen-age faith, before eleven years and three kids' worth of laundry, groceries, dirty diapers, putting food in their mouths, breakfast lunch and dinner, never an occasion for the silver. Long nights of waiting for him to come home reeking of bourbon. Still, her mother was right about one thing—silver is necessary. And today, it will mean cash in her hand, the first month's rent, a shot at a decent beginning.

MOVING

It's just a separation, their mother says, slamming the door on their old green house, on the built-in kitchen bench, the ruler giraffe Ryan and Callie measured themselves against, the steep hill of Gardner Street, Mr. and Mrs. Doody, the Little League ballpark, and their beagle, Babe. Babe is going to live on a farm where she can run free, and they are going to live in Barren. In Barren, their house will be an apartment building, which means you can visit your friends in the rain. This is what Ryan told Mr. and Mrs. Doody at their good-bye tea. Ryan drank lemonade from a china cup, and Mrs. Doody sewed a pearl on Chimp's chest so Ryan wouldn't forget them. Mr. Doody's garden was hoed in neat rows. He said Ryan's name would appear in their prayers. Ryan promised to remember them.

Now the door closes and Tessa sits in Callie's lap waving bye-bye to nobody. Ryan holds Chimp, and Callie wiggles Tessa's feet. How far away is Barren?

Try to memorize everything, Callie says.

Because she is older, she has made up a game for memory. Say a list backward and forward so you won't forget it. Babe, backyard, swingset, our house, Daddy. Daddy, our house, swingset, backyard, Babe. But Ryan can't keep it straight; there is too much to take to Barren. Mr. and Mrs. Doody, the flagpole, the ditch where the turtles crawled across wild strawberries, their father's lawn mower left in the garage, the front porch where the loose boards creaked. What is Barren?

Will Dad know where to find us? Ryan asks, trying to memorize the dandelions growing in the sidewalk's cracked cement.

He'll know if he's looking.

Desire

THE BARREN APARTMENTS

The apartment building is a box of curiosities. Every door has a number, and behind each door voices mix without meaning. Callie and Ryan walk the hallways, listening for a dark secret, but most of the words are just TV. In 308, Delores talks to her baby like a cartoon mouse, high and squeaky. Every day she wears huge, colored dresses that sway across her body. When Delores walks, elephants and palm trees rock in an earthquake. Sometimes a man in a dirty white T-shirt comes for Delores' baby. Callie and Ryan watch from the parking lot. Visitation, Callie says, a word she has heard her mother say. Behind the blinds, Delores stands waving, her body broken into thin strips.

In the apartment next to Delores, a tall, homely man plays the same song over and over. Earl, Delores screams out the open window, turn that crap down before I call the landlord. My baby's napping.

Delores and Earl ought to get married, Callie tells Ryan. They're perfect.

Sometimes the blonde woman from 303 carries out trash in her curlers and nightgown, sheer pink fabric transparent in the summer sun.

In the parking lot the tenants pass without speaking, but each face has a number and each number a closed door. The parking lot melts into soft blacktop; hot stones stick to their bare feet. This is Ryan's last summer without a shirt, and her back and belly bake into a warm caramel.

Past the parking lot are woods, waiting to be the next building. Ryan teaches Callie how to curve her toes into the bark and climb trees. Before Barren, Ryan never taught Callie anything. Behind thick leaves, they sit and spy and make up stories. In the woods, they are orphans of a pioneer family.

Don't cry, Callie says. We can take care of ourselves, we don't need anybody.

She sends Ryan to collect poison berries and whistles her back when it's time to eat. Purple berries melt in Ryan's moist palms, and the juice seeps between her fingers like blood from a wound. Tall weeds whip across their legs, burning their skin, and in their ears there's the sharp hiss of insects buzzing.

Under an old board of a tree fort, they hide two shoe boxes. In one, Ryan keeps a snake named Sammy. In the other, Callie saves money for someday. The two boys from 107, Clyde and Jerry, are hunters scouting the woods for squirrel meat. Through the thick grass they prowl, their B.B. guns cocked, anxious for prey. They show the girls how to target shoot at tin cans, and Callie wants a gun for her birthday.

We're gathering supplies for survival. You don't know how long it'll be before we're rescued, Callie tells Ryan, counting out her share of the pennies.

I don't want to live with another family, Ryan says, giving Callie back the money. If we're found, do you think they'll take me away from you?

No, Callie says. I'd never let them separate us. Trust me.

Compared to The Barren Apartments, the small green house of the marriage was boring: Too many days on the same swingset, watching caterpillars spin threads in a pickle jar, their own yard a prison of safety. Why were they sad to leave? Here, in Barren, there are so many doors waiting to open into mysteries.

NIGHT

Headlights walk through the bedroom window like private eyes, carefully inching light over the empty walls, hoping to uncover the face of a sleeping baby, then leaving. Callie listens for the slammed door of her mother's Ford, the car that promised to be home early. Over her head, footsteps from the second floor crack across the ceiling, a line of sound that shivers down the walls and into Callie's bed. Sometimes the line turns into a man, leaning in the doorway. But then the headlights come back, and the man disappears with the shadow.

Because she is ten, she can take care of the family. Ten is old enough to understand a marriage going bad and people doing what it takes to keep going. This is what he told her that day, snapping the latch on his suitcase. Take care of your sisters for me. Her sisters are young and asleep. Callie is trying to hold the family together with her hands, but most days it is too big. *Bye baby bunting, Daddy's gone a hunting*, Callie sings Tessa to sleep. And Ryan hides in a corner, curled into a ball behind a high wall of pillows and stuffed animals. It is a big job being a father, and Callie doesn't know how to do it any better. What if a clue never comes?

The air in the apartment hangs thick with the heat of summer. Callie is sure she can't breathe. Her body sweats on top of the tangled sheets. Shoes tap past her window and stop. When the summer ends, they will sleep with the windows shut. When the summer ends, school will be a new place and maybe she won't know what they're studying. At Our Lady of the Lake, she was top of her class in subtracting, an expert at guessing what was left when you took something away. At Our Lady of the Lake, she was chosen to be May Queen, carrying lilacs to the feet of the

Virgin Mary. Would her new teacher at Redemption be like Sister Ursula? Sister Ursula told Callie she could see things in her soul other people couldn't see. She said Callie could still be holy, even though her parents were divorcing. But now she would miss Confirmation with the rest of her class. What was Confirmation anyway? A new name and a new dress. Sister said it was no great gift that Callie was pretty. When a girl is poor, beauty can spell trouble with a capital T. Looks are easy to parade, but they can't steer you straight.

Ryan wakes up and screams for Callie. She has done this every night since they moved to Barren, and every night Callie has carried her back into bed for a story. Rolling her body against Ryan, Callie begins the same story. A cat named Sophie gets stuck in a tree and crawls up to heaven. Her owners cry in the world below, but God is happy. Ryan's wet cheek soaks through Callie's pajamas, a damp circle on Callie's chest, and in her arms Ryan's tiny body quivers like a baby sparrow's wing. Between the surprise of headlights, the room fills up with a darkness so powerful not even a good father could make it go away.

THE PHONE

Shirl curls hair at The Barren Beauty Boutique and lives in 303. Pink chairs, a satin bedspread and a color TV make Shirl's apartment a department-store luxury.

Alimony, Shirl says, when the girls tell her they've never met a woman this rich before. This summer, Shirl is their mother's best friend. Callie and Ryan haven't made real friends with anybody, and they wonder about their new mother, so eager and easy.

At the apartment pool, Shirl paints her toenails bright red, stuffing cotton balls between each toe to help them dry properly. Pedicures. Shirl was schooled in these. Cuticle trims, too. Skin that creeps over your nails like weeds and must be kept back.

When the beauticians are bored at The Barren Beauty Boutique, Shirl changes her hair color. No one, not even Shirl, remembers the original. Who cares, Shirl says. Now it is bright white and rolled into a neat underflip. Blondes belong tan, Shirl says, smoothing Q.T. cream over her orange body.

Shirl and their mother push their plastic chairs together, trade secrets behind greasy hands. The smell of coconut oil and chlorine hang in the heat. In the corner, covered by a clear box, the black telephone hides from the water sneaking down the concrete. The only tenants who own a pool phone, Shirl and their mother tell the others it's just for emergencies. But all day they wait for the phone to ring, then take turns flirting with men they've met or hope to meet. Shirl calls the phone a divorcée's necessity. Between rings they sing to Callie's transistor radio, tuned to KTYE. *We Gotta Get Out of This Place* is Shirl's favorite song, and she pronounces each word like an urgent message. No one else can touch the phone. The phone is for Ladies Only.

When she runs in for chips and pitchers of ice tea, rubber sandals snap against the calloused soles of Shirl's feet.

Be careful not to splash the cigarettes, Shirl yells as the girls race past.

Take some chips and go play, their mother says. We need our privacy.

At the shallow end, Tessa floats in the center of a green frog. Pretend there are lily pads and fairies underneath, Ryan tells Tessa.

The voices on the phone are a mystery, more friends than Ryan or Callie can ever imagine meeting.

Barren is just a bad movie without an ending, Shirl says, hanging up angry.

Forget it, their mother says. This isn't eternity.

Does that mean we're moving again? Ryan asks Callie.

It doesn't matter now, Callie says. We can swim the length without life preservers; that's something we'll keep.

BOBBY BRADY

When Bobby Brady returns from the war, his dog tags
jingle on his bare summer chest. He wears his own and
one from his best buddy, McDaniels, who wasn't so lucky.
There but for the grace of God, he says, lifting them to his
lips for a quick kiss.

Bobby Boy, their mother and Shirl call him, because
of his smooth wide face and the way he tickles their feet.
Bobby drinks beer from a big brown bottle, killer quarts,
and spits out the last swallow. Like squirrel piss, he says.

The silver medals, a mirror of the sun, thrill Ryan,
thrill her like Bobby's voice with the radio, low and knowing every word. Next to the pool, Bobby lies face down
on the burning concrete while Ryan tugs at the soft blond
curls in the curve of his back.

Aren't you hot, Bobby?

Hell, no. After Vietnam, Barren is easy.

When Ryan asks about the war, Bobby says it will be
over before she's old enough to know it's happening.

Did you meet Evelyn's father over there?

No, no, Bobby says. The jungle is a big place.

Ryan molds her toes into Bobby's shoulders, balances
above the deep water, a circus act. He is teaching her flips,
backward and forward, and her stomach rolls in fast circles
like love.

I'd marry your mother tomorrow if she'd take me,
Bobby says, leading Ryan's arms around his neck. Her legs
hug his hard stomach. Now hold on to me, he says, jumping off the board, sky diving.

The chlorine stings Ryan's eyes, but through the blue
she sees Bobby's lips puckered into a fish kiss.

Bobby, I'll take you, Ryan says, breaking the water to

breathe. Wait for me. I'm a mermaid.

Oh, please, her mother says, the voice a slap in the face of a dream. I can't believe it's started already.

RODEOS

Dean rides bulls bareback, which means he's brave.
From the bleachers they watch his denim shirt rock madly
above the dirt. One arm flies free, a dance of balance.
When he falls the crowd gasps, and the man on the
loudspeaker announces the time Dean held on. Lately,
Dean has promised Callie a palomino horse and a farm
house with a field if he's her new father. He knows how to
sketch ponies to look real, and he taught Callie how to
feather the mane with soft, loose pencil strokes. But he has
a mean streak too. He makes them eat pepper on their
steak. Callie waits for him to come up from the dirt and
wishes both ways, for a horse and for Dean to be hurt. But
he always gets up, shakes off the dust and walks away.
Older kids come by selling hot dogs and pink cotton candy. Her mother sits in the stands smiling, buying them
treats with Dean's money, rubbing a kleenex damp with
spit across the girls' faces. Sometimes she hoots a sweet
yoohoo and waves at another lady a few seats away.
Yoohoos embarrass Callie.

At night their apartment becomes a club of real
cowboys, and Sunday mornings the living room floor is a
collection of worn boots, beer cans and Dean's friends
sleeping. Quietly, Callie and Ryan dress Tessa for 8:30
Mass. When they come back, a few cowboys are left, rolling cigarettes and drinking Bloody Marys. They always
make a puzzle of the night before, putting together a story
from patches of memory. Laughter slides under the
bedroom door, morning mysteries of their mother and
Dean. Win or lose, the cowboys say, you pay for the rodeo
Sunday morning. Callie agrees.

THE PARADE

Crêpe paper weaves between the spokes, and when the wheels of the Schwinn spin, the clothespinned playing cards sound like fingers snapping. Threads of ribbon stream out of the handlebars, purple, thin ribbons like ringlets in a Shirley Temple movie. Tenants in the apartment parking lot pass by with suggestions on how to win—tape on pennies, dangle jingle bells from the seat—and Callie tries everything. At the summer playground parade, Callie's bike will be the envy of every girl who has whispered against her. This summer, Callie will be the winner. And Callie has something else, a costume for herself, her dance recital outfit from the old house.

Inside the apartment, Ryan helps Callie unpack the white straw cowboy hat. The hat turns Callie into a girl from the old West. Beaded strings swing loose across her neck. Callie steps into her leotard; pink sequins flash in even rows like scales of a magical fish. Because it is hot, Callie will ride without her tights. But the best thing will be a pair of short, white cowboy boots with fringe around the tops that waves when Callie walks. Ryan runs for her mother's lipstick and Callie stands with her chin tilted. I'm going to win.

Tim runs the summer playground program, and Callie is in love with him. He is sixteen, but not too old for Callie. When he taught them to make sculptures from copper wire, Callie twisted out a large heart for him. Now he calls Callie his honey, and of all the kids he says Callie is his one and only. Today she will ride by him in her cowboy suit, the sequins dazzling in the afternoon sun, and he will award her the ribbon, the only one, first place. Just last year she was the May Day Queen, but here in Barren, people think she's nobody. A girl without a father. She has

38

a father, but people don't treat her that way. That's why today she must ride, cards clicking all the way, the movie star of the parade, and on her feet the white fringe of the boots will catch the wind and sway. The ribbon will be tacked on her wall. When school starts, everyone will hear about her ahead of time. Like her father's eyes, Tim's eyes will glow with adoration and pride.

Ryan gives Callie the lipstick, watches as she transforms her thin lips into full, pink flowers. I hope it's a long time before Tim marries you, she says, afraid a man will take Callie early.

You'll come, too, Callie says, tucking the lipstick into her leotard. You're my sister. Sisters don't forget.

THE MISTAKE

Upstairs in 310, Earl's records are stacked in the wire rack, alphabetically, by artist, so Earl knows what he's reaching for. Callie jiggles the 45 out of its neat jacket. Careful with your fingers, Earl warns. One print can ruin a record.

A bachelor pad, Earl calls his apartment, now that he lives there alone. On Sundays, chocolate gifts are carried to the nursing home, treats for Earl's mother, stolen early by a stroke. Most days she doesn't remember Earl's name; the hours are used up by an old argument with Earl's dead father, but Earl doesn't complain.

Who knows where the mind goes, Earl tells Callie. It's a bad rap, getting old.

Papered in postcards, Earl's kitchen looks like a mixed-up travel package. A cartoon sketch of a fisherman with a mermaid catch, an orange sunset over sparkling water, a tan blonde in a skimpy bikini — these are some of the pictures that keep Earl company.

Everywhere we went, Earl says, Mother insisted on sending postcards home. That way, when we got back, our mailbox was full, and we could relive our trip like it was someone else's.

With his large ears, crooked hook nose, Earl is the night rider from Sleepy Hollow. Long hair fringes his lanky neck. The latest craze, Earl says. I'm finally able to do my own thing without my mother nagging. On the night shift, Earl vacuums the carpeting at KTYE, his record collection a sampling of D.J.s' extras. I take whatever they give me. *Playing solitaire till dawn, with a deck of fifty-one*, Earl croons his favorite tune, lifts the needle to begin again. *Smoking cigarettes and watching Captain Kangaroo, now don't tell me, I've nothing to do.*

40

Saturday mornings, Earl and Callie lounge in beanbag chairs for Bandstand; they rate hits, score the dancers. We're going to be next, Earl says, pulling her to her feet for dance practice. They prepare for the day they will dance in front of millions with The Dirty Dog and The Swim, the numbers Earl knows best. We could be winners, kid, Earl tells Callie.

Callie knows Earl will never get that far, but she lets him teach her anyway. After Bandstand, they study the photos in Earl's high school yearbook, the smiles of Eisenhower students repeated in snapshots. Sometimes, for a game, Callie opens the book and picks a face, and Earl must tell her the stranger's story. Five years after graduation, Earl still remembers a little bit about everybody.

I spent a lot of time watching, Earl explains. He likes the photo of the Pepfest of '63 when the whole football team masqueraded as cheerleaders. Balloons for boobs, Earl tells Callie.

But she doesn't want to hear private words about bodies.

Tell me about your best friend, Callie says, to change the subject.

I didn't have too many buddies. I really just hung out with my mom and my Chevy. Earl's car is his bankroll on wheels, his hot rod, his best broad.

Earl begs Callie to come out cruising. But her mother says no. If you ask me, that Earl is questionable.

She'll never find out, Earl tells Callie, flipping the 45. We can go before she gets home, it'd be cool. I need a pretty girl to ride beside me.

Okay, Callie says. It might as well be her.

In the car, Callie runs her fingers through the matted purple fur of Earl's seat covers.

Listen to this, Earl says, charging the motor into a roaring machine gun. Tilted high off the ground, the

Chevy's trunk bounces over the backroads of Barren. From the rear-view mirror, Earl's graduation tassel swings.

Let's crank that radio, Earl says, and *Born to Be Wild* blasts out the open window.

The hot rush of August wind splashes back Callie's hair. There is a wild freedom in speed and her face out the open window.

Callie, Earl says, run away with me.

On the dashboard, the head of a circus clown bobs, his coiled neck disappearing into a cheery belly. Of course, we'd have to hide from the police, Earl stutters. You're jailbait, you know that, don't you? Guys my age can't tie up with young girls, even if they are as pretty as you. Hey, why don't I spin you by Lovers' Lane; that's where all the fast guys took their dates.

Earl, I have to get back, Callie says, or else you'll be in real trouble.

The clown chuckles at Earl's mistake. Someday she will run away, shed Barren like the useless skin of a snake, but not with a man who is Ichabod Crane.

WILD RIVER DAYS

The words Harley, Yamaha, Kawasaki arrive like foreign countries. The first night of the fair, the bikers storm their choppers over the roof of the liquor store.

Even the cops are scared, the clerk at Ben Franklin tells Callie. You kids better be careful. Those Hell's Angels have kidnapped a hundred girls like you. If it were up to me, Wild River Days would be history.

But Callie and Ryan love the fair. They twirl on the Scrambler over and over, flying close to a screaming face; then in an instant, the faces change.

In the arcade, the Hell's Angels throw hoops over the thin necks of bottles, shoot at moving ducks, toss dimes onto glass plates. They capture every prize: velvet paintings, blow-up beer bottles and huge, stuffed teddy bears. Ryan wants a big animal for her collection, but she knows she'll never win.

If we're nice to the bikers, Callie says, we'll get one, easy.

The girls smile at every biker carrying a bear. A skinny man with a rose tattoo winks back at Callie.

Aren't you a regular dirty beauty. What can I do for you, honey? he asks, his few teeth crooked and black. Call me Crash.

Crash buys Callie a blue sno-cone and Ryan gets one, too.

Where'd you win that bear? Callie asks, petting the animal's short, pink fur.

This thing? Shit, you can have it, honey. It's yours for a kiss.

Crash kneels down and Callie brushes her lips against his, quick. That bargain fell in my favor, kid, Crash says, and gives her the bear.

When Crash disappears into the crowd, Callie tells Ryan, I got it for you. Stuffed animals don't interest me.

Ryan names the bear Crash, as a souvenir, and scratches behind his floppy ear.

DESIRE

The circus seals on her daughters' summer pajamas never drop their balls. And now her girls are asleep in the back seat, after begging their way on her first drive-in date with Dean. The shouts from a crowd of shaggy-haired kids scratch through the speaker, and on the screen a businessman is taken hostage by hippies and carried off to a tropical island where everyone runs around in guru robes, half-naked. It's a good thing her daughters have their own dreams to keep them company.

God, Dean says. This hippie shit makes me sick.

Here at the drive-in, young couples in cars are frantic from kissing, this crazy movie lost to bodies embraced in wet heat. Mosquitoes fly through the open windows and bite bare skin. Tomorrow one of these teen-age girls will soak in a hot bath and tie her hair up in a way that makes her look womanly. And maybe her date will pull up front the next night, or maybe he'll pass her by on the street like a stranger. But later her days begin with a wrenching gag, and the game is over. And maybe the girl gets married, but that doesn't make her lucky.

The world is a peculiar place when you are a mother; passion stays the way you remember but too far away to own it. She will explain all this to her daughters someday. The way the taffeta prom dresses and cashmere sweaters of her own boarding school days disappeared in another back seat, years away. It was a bad trade, cashing in large possibilities for a small house and three babies. Her daughters will be smarter, redeemed by her own mistakes. These days without cash, without anything, will pass, and she'll give them the necessities: painting classes, piano, private schools and French. But now they are asleep, with the seal's nose balancing the striped ball perfectly. There will be rules against drive-in movies. Wait a few years and all this will be on TV.

They're out, Dean says, motioning toward the back seat. Propping the bucket of popcorn on the dashboard, he fills her mouth with the warm butter of his tongue.

Desire belongs to girls who don't know any better. I'm too old, she tells Dean.

He laughs, but she isn't joking.

On the screen, the hippies dance in a circle, chanting. One day America changed, and she didn't catch it happening.

Surviving

SURVIVING

Far from Barren, the big white house by the water is home to their father, and also to a steady, mysterious Downbeat customer. The customer will miss the party; kids get under the customer's skin, but Callie would like to meet the person who takes their place as family.

A hot, damp blanket of air arrives with Callie's birthday. Calm before the storm, dad says, but the men keep drinking. There was no one else to invite but his friends, Track and McKee. McKee twists balloons into wiener dogs, a magic trick, nickels pulled from behind his ear, dollars slipping out his shirt sleeve. In another stunt, he makes a bottle of beer disappear in one drink. Callie opens her present, a reel-to-reel tape recorder, but none of the men can make it work.

You figure it out another time, her dad tells her. Right now you better get your eye back on your baby sister. She's awfully close to joining that lake.

Callie snatches Tessa away from the water, carries her, fighting, back to the center of the birthday party.

I can listen to that at home, Track says. Can't a guy just drink in peace?

Quiet her down, will you honey? her dad tells Callie.

But the men decide it's time to leave. I got better things to do with my day besides babysitting, Track says.

Happy birthday, you old lady, McKee tells Callie. And try to keep those boys away.

Ryan, get me a diaper, Callie orders, while Tessa struggles to get away.

Isn't that your job, Daddy? Track yells as the car pulls away.

Tessa's skin, clammy with sweat, soaks through Callie's sundress.

Why isn't that baby toilet trained? her father asks, angry.

In the sky, the clouds gather low and gray. Nothing moves, not even the water on the lake. We're in for it, he says. This is the way it starts. Callie collects the cake, the tape recorder, Tessa's diaper bag. Take what you want to save, he says. In an hour this scene will be history.

Ryan bundles Teddy and Chimp in Tessa's quilt. Ryan, for Christ's sake, you're too old for those, he says, his words heavier than the heat.

Leave her alone, Callie says. She's not as old as me.

Cool and silent, his basement room is a relief from the heat. It's easy and cheap, that's why I live here, her father says, surrounded by walls of cement squares. It's not the Ritz, he tells them, but it's all I need.

Outside, the rain starts with the hard and sudden sound of stones thrown against the window. Hail, he says. If we put a pail outside the door, we can see some. A rush of wind sweeps the hail in through the open door; small white balls scatter across the floor. This is it, he says. Feel it.

What for? Callie asks.

For the memory, he says, rolling the hail in his hands. You're living through something you've never seen.

Thunder booms, the lights blink, then surrender completely. That's it for electricity, he says, fumbling through the dark for his transistor radio. The damn batteries are dead, he says. This storm is going to do a number. The best we can do is guess.

Tessa cries. She's hungry, Callie says. We didn't even get a chance to eat.

There's cake and cold hot dogs, he says. This isn't the time to start cooking.

Pacing the floor, Callie jiggles Tessa, but Tessa still

screams. Do something with that baby, he tells Callie. I can't take that screeching.

The storm has turned the day to night. Why's it so dark already? Ryan asks, cradling Teddy and Chimp in her lap.

It's tornado time, ladies. Start praying.

What's a tornado? Ryan asks.

It's a funnel that sucks up everything. Cars, people, houses. You name it, it takes it. All we can do now is get on our knees and rattle those beads.

He drags a chair to the window, climbs up, looks out. The clouds are whipping across the lake now, he says. Get down.

Faces pressed against the cold linoleum, they listen to the crash of glass, the crunch of tree limbs breaking.

You know the Our Father, he says. Get going.

Loud rumble, the house shakes, a window cracks, a sheet of rain drenches their praying bodies. Callie covers Tessa, Ryan screams.

Hang on, he says, if you can get through this, you can survive anything.

It's clear, he says, when the silence sets in. Get up and see. You go first. Lifting Callie to his shoulders he holds her up to the broken window.

Can you see anything?

There is a tree like a net with the day's catch. A cat wrapped around a branch, the bars of a swingset, a nest of wire.

Let me down. I've seen enough, Callie says. When's Mom coming?

Who knows, he says. You were supposed to spend your birthday with me.

THE TRUCK STOP

Saturdays, Darlene the babysitter makes beds at the Stagecoach Truck Stop. Callie and Ryan wait for this day, the dirty ashtrays and crumpled sheets. Darlene has taught them to tuck in the corners properly, tight triangles, so the bedclothes are nice and stiff for the next guy. Darlene's boyfriend, Craig, is a trucker, and she prepares each room as if Craig were the next customer.

You'll do it for your own man someday, she tells the girls.

Lifting the toilet seat, she shows them how to search for hidden germs and yellow stains of old pee. In some rooms the girls find magazines with full-fleshed bodies of naked ladies.

Centerfolds, Darlene says when they spread the pictures out on the bed to study. Better close those up. We know what it's about, we have our own bodies.

The girls collect matchbook covers from far away, and sometimes, when they're lucky, loose change. When Callie can, she slips the money into her pocket without Darlene knowing. Ryan loves matchbooks; she imagines highways stretching across a desert and arriving in a new place. Darlene keeps the magazines for Craig. The rooms smell of cigarette butts, gasoline, men's shaving cream, sweaty skin on dirty sheets. But all the rooms they clean are empty, the guests a case of missing bodies.

After work, Darlene gets them free Cokes in the truck stop café, and they sit in the orange booth, watching men bend over coffee mugs and heavy white plates. Callie makes up a game, guessing which ones left their money and which ones slept with the pictures of naked ladies.

The girls have discovered the men's secret identities. All of the men have abandoned their families; their wives searched at first, then gave up looking. And their children play in sandboxes, pushing toy trucks they now call Daddy.

DUTY

Evelyn's father fights for freedom in another country. Evelyn's mother waits for Evelyn's father to come home. Doing his duty, she tells the girls, her eyes jumping behind the stern rims of her thick glasses. It is not at all the same situation as with your father. She allows them the ridiculous round-tipped scissors. Don't hurt yourselves.

Evelyn's father serves his country. From a gold frame, Evelyn's father watches over their days, serious about his duty. His medals and ribbons mean honor and bravery.

Callie cuts out a school dress for Betsy McCall, the paper doll. Water runs in crystal balls down the window; Betsy will need a slicker, too. Because Evelyn is just six, they only play with her when it rains. Callie says Ryan can play at Evelyn's any day, but Ryan won't go without Callie. Quiet as a cloud, Evelyn reminds Callie of a gray day. Her thin braids rest like dead grass on her back.

Evelyn remembers him. Don't you, Evelyn?

Evelyn bites her lower lip and nods, yes.

A thick book without pictures rests in Evelyn's mother's lap. I'm trying to make something of myself, in case Vietnam drags on longer than we expect.

Their apartment is a safe oven of pot roast and cinnamon cookies. In the evenings, the smell of Evelyn's dinner lingers in the hallways. Just once, Callie and Ryan want to stay for supper, but Evelyn's mother never asks.

When I moved into the Barren Apartments—she takes off her glasses and kneads the knuckle of her thumb into her eye —I never thought I'd live among these types. Evelyn's father would certainly not approve. As soon as he's out, we'll get a house in a neighborhood with good families. This situation is just temporary. For us anyway.

Of course, nobody blames you girls for your upbringing. Evelyn's life will be splendid once her father comes back.

Betsy McCall's wardrobe is immense — three pairs of shoes, a tam for school, a leather satchel, three ruffled pinafores. It's temporary for us, too, Callie says, slipping the scissors over Betsy's foot and slicing it off.

It was true what their mother told them: In an apartment, you can visit your friends in the rain. But it rains, just the same.

FIRST GRADE

On the bulletin board, the reading kites inched toward the sky. Every book read was another inch, and in the end, Ryan's kite reached the sky first. The award was hers, a white glass statue of the Virgin Mary's head.

At night, Ryan caresses the Virgin's face to keep the nightmares away. Into her dreams she mumbles, *Hail Mary full of grace the Lord is with thee.*

But then a classmate's mother, Mrs. Randolf, stands in Redemption's hallway. Hands on her hips, eyebrows pinched into a severe line, she tells Sister that no one can read faster than her daughter, Suzy. She says the contest is a lie.

Sister Angela sweeps her frightening black sleeve over Ryan's head and says, You belong out in the hallway. This discussion pertains to you directly. Sister is very fond of the word *pertain*. If it doesn't pertain, you are a busybody.

Ryan's classmates twist in their chairs, a full theatre turned on Ryan's hot face.

Did she really read all those books? Really? Does she have any proof? Isn't there only her mother at home and isn't she always working? Mrs. Randolf finds it funny for a girl like that to read so fast. She has sat with Suzy through each book, can vouch for Suzy's speed. Can Ryan's mother claim the same thing?

No, Ryan knows she can't.

But, Sister insists, Ryan is in the top reading group, one of the best.

Mrs. Randolf says her daughter, Suzy, should be at the head of the class. I think this little girl is playing a trick.

Suzy smiles, and her teeth remind Ryan of the German shepherd on the path to school, growling.

Mrs. Randolf demands a title and the full story of each

book Ryan has read. Ryan tries to remember, but her mind is stuck on a monkey named Pete who hides under his bed every morning.

I want the Virgin back until it's settled, Mrs. Randolf says.

Sister orders Ryan to return Mary promptly.

Now Ryan stays in bed with the Virgin's head held tight against her floating heart. Sister Angela sends reading worksheets and an apology home with Callie, but she still needs the prize returned immediately. Ryan listens to no one but Mary.

Tell Sister you dropped it and Mary cracked, Callie says. That way they'll never get her back.

But Mary knows it isn't fair, and Ryan's other mother doesn't care about kites reaching the sky first.

BARREN BITUMINOUS

The tiny rocks pile into steep hills, and children who crawl on them are swallowed under and smothered to death. Later they become a part of the blacktop and cars roll, without knowing, across their bodies. Ray, their mother's boss, warns the girls with this story and watches from the shack to make sure they play far enough away. A huge, rough-whiskered man, Ray gives them money and stashes boxes of Milk Duds for them in his top desk drawer. Every gift requires a kiss. Ray's rough face is fire on their cheeks.

On Saturdays, when the place is empty, Ray, leaning on the front loader, blows *When Irish Eyes Are Smiling* on his harmonica. Ryan and Callie have learned all the words and while Ray plays, they sing. Between jokes that are a puzzle, Ray's laugh is harsh and low and bumpy. Inside the dusty gray office, their mother sits all day, punching numbers into a heavy green machine, numbers that fall out on streams of paper, numbers that keep Barren Bituminous ahead of the game. Sometimes she walks to the window for a wave or opens the door and scolds them with a strict voice, warning, Watch out for the rocks.

The dust from unlaid roads covers their clothes, sifts into their skin in fine webs of dirt. Mice dart between the heaps of stones and the girls chase after them, screaming. Ryan collects dull rocks shaped like clouds, or boats, or the moon's face. The rocks turn into characters in her stories. She gives them voices, chatty and winding.

Ray lifts Callie to the top of the bulldozer and hands Tessa to her. Callie pretends to shift while Tessa steers.

So, where in the hell are you broads going?

We're running away. Don't tell anybody.

Ray spits the dust off his tongue. Have a good trip, take it easy.

At Barren Bituminous, the dirt and dust and stones wait to grow into roads. Someday the girls will follow the blacktop to another place, but today they are like the rocks in Ryan's hands, too small to leave.

PANCAKE BREAKFAST

Callie pours the batter onto the thick flat skillet. At the edges of the circles, the liquid rolls into tiny yellow beads, beads that sizzle, turn black. The wooden spoon in Ryan's fist spins against the heavy batter, breaks through the bubbles. Ryan watches the airholes form and disappear. Fathers and daughters couple in the hot kitchen, cooking pancakes for the Parish Pancake Breakfast. Ryan stands on the stepladder and stares at them. Callie brought Ryan in place of their father. Callie's certain grip mans the spatula, lifts the pancakes, flips. Golden skin stretches tight on the warm underside. Out in the Parish Hall, dabs of soft butter melt on the parishioners' plates and the syrup merges into it, sweet.

The fathers all have short haircuts and wear glasses, brown-rimmed and serious. White shirts and ties are tucked behind clean aprons.

How come Dad never wears a tie? Ryan asks.

Callie answers loud and fast, taking Ryan's bowl of batter away. He wears them every day, dummy.

Reaching to claim the batter back, Ryan knows better. Never. Not for church. Bermuda shorts and slippers. Never to work. What did he wear, then? Golf shirts. All the same golf shirts, short-sleeved with penguins on the pockets. But never a tie. Ryan is sure of her memory.

Do you think if Dad knew about the breakfast he would have come today?

Callie's eyes narrow, tight and angry. I think I better take over the pancakes. You're too young to understand anything. Of course Dad would come, but he's away on business, making a lot of money. He's coming home with skateboards for both of us and a diamond ring for Mom on their anniversary.

The last pancake on the skillet smokes, the skin a crisp black, burning. Some of the fathers and daughters are watching.

My sister doesn't understand anything, Callie tells the fathers. The fathers look away.

Ever since school started, Callie shifts into queer stories, stories she wants Ryan to repeat, but Ryan doesn't know the rules. Opening the stack of pancakes in the middle, Callie slips the black one in, hidden on top by ones that are perfectly golden. She delivers the plate to one of the fathers.

Here you go, they're ready.

Digging her fingernails into Ryan's wrist, Callie says, That's right, isn't it? Do you understand me?

THE BICYCLE

Ryan's father drives up with a bicycle in a cardboard box. This year Ryan's birthday party will have to be in the apartment parking lot. It's a long story, but he's sorry. He grinds out his cigarette with the scuffed toe of his black loafer. On the hood of the car, Callie is caught in his arms.

Well, open it, honey, he tells Ryan. It's your birthday.

Ripping into the heavy brown wrapping, Ryan spies the red and silver shine of freedom. Now she can ride beside Callie to school, to the store. Callie can't leave her at home anymore. After the training wheels come off, she will tie Chimp to the back fender and ride home to her old neighborhood, the kind house of Mr. and Mrs. Doody. Mr. Doody will be gloved, working in his garden. Ryan will hoe beside him while Mrs. Doody picks strawberries and tells stories of her dead dog, Ginger. There will be the sweet taste of dinner, cooked carrots, pickles and pork chops. Then the three of them will kneel on the living room rug, Mr. Doody leading the rosary. Maybe the new people would let her see her old house, the front porch with the loose boards, the basement where Babe slept next to her toy chest, her bedroom walls where the branches of trees twisted into monsters. Once, when she was afraid, her mother made animal shadows on the wall to prove darkness was friendly. But that was before Barren.

Ryan sets the sleek handlebar in her lap, her journey a secret she will only tell Callie.

Callie is reading directions. I'll help you, Daddy.

Ryan's mother opens the building door, angry. Hey, I could call the police right now if I wanted to. I told you if you want to see my kids, you call and ask me.

Ryan's father puts the screwdriver in his shirt pocket and leans against his car, easy but mean.

Give me a break, Joan. It's for Ryan's birthday.

So? her mother says. What happened to birthday parties at your place?

The last one didn't work out too great, he says, trading his toothpick for another cigarette. He brushes his hand over Callie's hair.

But you want to call the shots, you get the kid a bike this year. He tugs the handlebar away from Ryan, drops the cardboard box back into the trunk. Like I said, I'm sorry, honey. He kisses Ryan's forehead. I love you, sweet baby. Birthdays are bummers, anyway.

Callie whispers in his ear and he reaches into his pocket, passes her a wad of wrinkled dollars. Whatever you need.

Ryan can't watch her bike leave. Mom, she begs. Can't the bike stay?

Christ, he'll keep the bike for you, don't worry. Besides, you're not going anywhere today.

DEER

Under their mother's sunglasses, a blue swamp circles one eye and seeps down her cheek. Callie opens the bottle of Cover Girl Creamy Ivory and says, Dean.

Her mother's head shakes no to a tired beat, but Callie knows she's lying.

I can't go to work today, let Ray fire me.

Callie dabs the Creamy Ivory on her fingertips, blends the make-up into her mother's skin, white and thin as tissue wrapping. You're not going to miss work again, Callie says, setting the sunglasses on the sink soapdish. But the bruise shows through. These days, her mother's breath is a potion of gasoline and onions frying.

Now she cowers on the toilet, tears falling on her bony knees. Callie watches the sharp wings of her shoulders rise and fall.

Why did he do this to me? From her crib, Tessa screams. I can't be everything to everybody.

Today Callie is supposed to be a baker in the fifth grade play, but her mother has forgotten to create a costume. Last night she promised Callie a puffy white hat and a baker's apron, before she left for the Oasis Tavern. Callie can't be in the play without a costume, but it doesn't matter anyway.

I'll call in for you. What do you want me to say?

Callie's mother turns the hot water on and off, watches it slither down the drain.

What do you want me to tell Ray about your face?

Say anything.

Ray's voice is rough and worried. Is there anything I can do? What happened exactly?

Callie says, The deer came out of nowhere, it bounced off the headlight and shattered the windshield. There wasn't time to stop or swerve. It happened with a friend, but only she was hurt.

Don't call me *she*, her mother cries from the bathroom.

She'll be okay in a couple of days, Callie tells Ray. You'll see.

And in Callie's mind, there is a deer on Highway 13, lying dead near the side of the road.

TERROR

The German shepherd snarls his lips away from his vicious teeth, and Ryan, seeing him hurl himself wildly against the wire fence, starts praying. *Jesus Mary and Joseph I give you my heart and my soul Jesus Mary and Joseph assist me now and in my last agony.* Today their mother is hurt, so Callie must stay home with her. For the first time this year, Ryan has to walk the path to school alone. Alone. The woods turn suddenly dangerous and the path narrow. The dog's bark is so terrifying and close, Ryan feels his teeth on the back of her neck. Blood pounds in her ears, her legs run automatically, trembling and weak. Ahead of her a man with a gun hides between trees. Trees of bare branches, skeletons of dead bodies. This morning thick clouds mask the sunlight, but sometimes for seconds Ryan's eyes are shocked by light. Callie says Ryan has to learn to get by without her; she says she won't always be there. Callie is wrong, but Ryan can't convince her. A loose root hooks the toe of Ryan's blue uniform shoe and she lands face against the ground, her mouth, chin and cheek smeared with dirt and new tears. Ryan wipes the salty mud from her lips. The wolf still howls, but he has not caught her. The man still lurks, he will lurk forever. Behind her, the teeth grow into a set of kitchen knives. Ahead of her, death wears the mask of a murderer. Ryan crawls off the path and into the weeds, a prickly plant needles into her knee. Callie will come looking or God's big hand will lift her out of the woods safely. Callie is wrong; Callie has to protect her. Ryan is a rabbit in a world of traps.

MRS. MEAR

Every day, on her way home from Barren Bituminous, she must pass Mrs. Mear's station wagon, slouched outside the Oasis Tavern. Across the street, Mrs. Mear's filthy sons balance two brown bags of groceries in the front baskets of their bikes. Hygiene must be a word those boys have never heard. What time does that woman start drinking? Breakfast, probably. A beer in place of cornflakes. And the boys, Clyde and Jerry, run wild morning to night, dangle upside down from the trees outside the apartment building. But they are good kids, good to her daughters. They have taught the girls the deadman's float and elegant backflips. Still, they are so dirty.

The other tenants talk against the family. Once, the crusted dishes were piled so high the plumber couldn't see his way to the sink. Yellowed sheets pass for curtains, giving a bad look to the whole building. There are times when their electricity is cut off and the hallways fill with the smoke of old wax. Trash collectors, pigs, the other tenants call them, but she can't join in.

Clyde and Jerry tell her daughters stories about their father working in another city. But Shirl has set her straight. Working means punching out license plates, doing time for armed robbery. A gas station holdup, no one hurt, but the gun was pointed right in the clerk's face. Shirl cherishes the gritty details of every crime committed in Barren.

Like father, like son, Shirl always tells her when she sees the girls playing with the boys. You can bet I wouldn't let those mongrels within a hundred feet of my kids. If I had them.

Don't you ever go in that apartment, she warns her

daughters. And don't ever let those boys touch you skin to skin.

At night, before she puts her girls to sleep, she checks their heads for lice that might jump off the boys and settle on them.

Images of Mrs. Mear interrupt her dreams. The Barren bridge is crumbling and Mrs. Mear wobbles on the edge, a weak hand reaching out for help. At the last minute, Mrs. Mear strangles her and they fall together into the deep river that waits to suck them both under.

She has never spoken to Mrs. Mear, who staggers by, silent, but once, through the open window, she caught a screech of anger meant for Clyde and Jerry. A widow's peak divides Mrs. Mear's forehead. Every day the same dress sacks the bones of her body. At night, the tired station wagon zigzags through the streets of Barren, but even the police let Mrs. Mear go free.

Sometimes in the Oasis Tavern, she hurries past Mrs. Mear slumped in the back booth. It isn't easy, she wants to tell Mrs. Mear, but you do what you have to do. At the bar, she feels the desperate eyes of Mrs. Mear burn into her, but when she looks back, the eyes are closed in sleep. Maybe Mrs. Mear hates her for the way the men of Barren have gathered around her. Maybe she hates her because her daughters are clean.

At least there are groceries going home now, probably paid for with the boys' paper route money. Their handlebars teeter under the weight of the brown bags. As she passes, she waves; she can afford to be friendly.

Witness

WITNESS

Green almond eyes, Helena's perfect face, peach lips
sliding over white teeth, the ring of the register bell, penny
candy in both hands, these are the things that draw Callie
to Barren Dairy. Helena's parents stock the shelves, their
round bodies bent over open boxes of canned ham and
toilet paper. When they stand, they heave a huge sigh to let
the customers know they are working. Barren Dairy is
right across the apartment parking lot, the tenants are their
best customers. It's not a place for real groceries. Their
mother always says you pay the price for convenience. But
odds and ends—candy, pizza, macaroni and cheese—are
fine sometimes. Helena's long crystal earrings dangle like
tears from a chandelier, the winter sun making prisms
across the dirty linoleum. Except for Helena, this would be
just another store, but Helena's beauty hauls the men in.
After school, perched on the stool behind the counter,
Helena winds the strands of her golden hair around her
fingers and stares out at the parking lot.

Tonight, Helena's parents Christmas shop in the city,
and in the back room between Salems, Helena confides
everything to Darlene. Helena hates Holy Angels
Academy, hates the long bus ride and the prudish girls.

I was just meant for bigger things, Helena says, tosses
her head lightly. Earrings rock against her cheek.

It's a look Helena's been perfecting, Darlene once ex-
plained to Callie, adding, she's a girl too full of her own
face. But tonight, Darlene wants confessions anyway.

I just have to get out of here, Helena whines.

I felt the same way senior year, Darlene says. Every
day dragged on forever. No matter how many classes I
cut, there was still the next day.

How is it being out? Helena asks, smoothing her

71

paisley miniskirt over her fishnet tights. Tonight Helena is dressed up for a date. Don't I look sexy?

Yes, Darlene says.

So, Helena says, do you feel like you're out of jail?

Exactly. That's why I came to Barren. I just had to get out from under my family.

Me too, Helena says, sweeping her arms over the stacked boxes. Look at this dump. It's so trashy. I can't believe I live in the back of a grocery store. But why would anyone come to Barren? I can't wait to get away. I just want to be a wild thing. Helena screams, flings her head forward until her long hair tangles; then the hair flies back, lands in a windswept mess.

You'll get your chance, Darlene says. Trust me.

Helena tosses the key ring to Callie. Go lock up, kid. We want to discuss something privately. You and your sister go raid the candy.

Ryan is out of the back room fast, but Callie hesitates. Candy is not what she came for.

Go on, Darlene says, sneaks Callie a wink, meaning, I'll tell you everything. Darlene does not keep juicy details from Callie. Darlene says every word between them is pillow talk, big secrets best friends keep.

Callie clicks the lock, listens to the hushed voices leading to something. Through the glass door, new snow turns the empty blacktop into a clean, white sheet. The apartment building, with its tiny squares of light, reminds Callie of a package too perfect to open.

Darlene and Helena giggle. Making pictures out of penny candy, Ryan sits in the aisle. Red-hot jaw breakers outline a Christmas stocking. Finger against her lips, Callie warns Ryan to be a quiet spy. Since Barren, they have become better than detectives on TV. This Christmas they have asked for walkie-talkies in order to investigate properly. Sometime you'll be sorry, their mother has warned, but the spy game is too interesting to abandon. Even Darlene can't resist a good mystery.

Through the slats of the swinging door, Callie watches Helena try smoke rings.

When he pulls up, Helena tells Darlene, hide behind the building.

We'll crouch behind the dumpster, Darlene says.

What about those kids? Helena asks. What if they say something?

Not those kids. They've seen everything.

Bucket seats, scarlet velour upholstery, Helena says, nibbling on her thumbnail. God, if you saw the inside of his car you'd know what I mean. I'm so tempted to go all the way. What would you do if you were me?

Well, he's not going to wait forever. I'm sure he has his pick of fruit. Get me?

Outside the snow drifts in heavier flakes. A small, red sports car parks. Callie recognizes the face behind the windshield: Mr. Lavelle, organizer of the pancake breakfast, passer of the 8:30 Mass collection plate. Why is he parked here in the dark? Snow tries to blanket his windshield, but the wipers reveal Mr. Lavelle, the glow of his cigar. Callie unlocks the door, twists her wrist in circles, motions for him to roll down his window.

We're closed, she shouts. You're too late.

Where's Helena?

Who are you talking to? Helena asks from the back room. Then she is at the door, angry. Why didn't you tell me he was here? Get that candy off the floor and get going, she snaps at Ryan.

Their coats, Darlene says, rushing to the back room to get them.

There's no time, Helena screams. They can carry them home. It's not that far. Helena shoves her hand into Darlene's back. Get out.

The lock of Barren Dairy clicks, the girls stand shivering against the brick.

Ryan won't go without putting on her coat. It's freezing, she says, her chin quivering.

Go, Helena snaps, or give me back the candy. Her hands stretch out, demanding. Give it up or get going.

We'll hurry, Darlene says. Don't worry.

Helena, how about it? Mr. Lavelle says.

The zipper on Ryan's jacket is stuck.

Remember if they call you, I'm sleeping, Helena yells to Darlene. Then she is climbing into the car, her miniskirt creeping up her trembling long legs.

Callie's eyes are steady on the red sports car.

What are you looking at? Helena screams from her window. Forget it, she says to Mr. Lavelle. She doesn't know you. Let's just get out of here.

I do, too, Callie yells.

Darlene grabs Callie's wrist, yanks her toward the apartment building.

Come here, Mr. Lavelle calls to Callie, his voice suddenly calm like a priest's. Come here, I need to speak with you.

But Callie stays frozen, her feet solid in the snow. If she runs now, her shoes will slip on the ice and Helena and Mr. Lavelle will see her slide, face down, against the wet blacktop.

Listen, you little brat, he says. If you open your mouth you'll answer to me. Mr. Lavelle speaks with the cigar clenched between his teeth. Sweet, burning tobacco drifts out the car window. The motor races. In the glare of headlights, Callie, Ryan and Darlene are pinned against the building, animals blinded by the shock of light.

Forget what you saw or you'll deal with me, Mr. Lavelle spits. The wheels skid black lines through the new snow.

Was that Mr. Lavelle? Ryan asks, her mittened hand tight around Callie's.

Callie knows what happens to the star witness. She can identify him, there is no mistake. But he has seen their faces, too. They need to keep his secret or no one is safe.

No, Callie tells Ryan. The less we know the better.

BRITISH COLUMBIA

There are roads in British Columbia their father needs
to build. For Christmas, he sends them a snapshot and
Canadian jumpers, scratchy wool dresses the color of fall
leaves. Tessa gets a stuffed grizzly. In the picture, he appears smaller than they remember, a small man lost in
mountain-sized Christmas trees. One hand holds a fish by
its belly, the other rests on the cap of a boy. Both of them
are smiling in the snow. His jacket, unzipped, reveals his
hill of stomach. Ryan remembers old nights sleeping on the
peak of his belly, her mind easy on the dark forest of his
chest. Does the boy in the picture sleep in her place? He
stands exactly like their father, one knee cocked forward,
his weight dropping on his back hip. Even his eyes are like
their father's, dark and looking into nowhere. The two of
them wear high green rubber boots that lace up the leg.

Callie reads Ryan the letter, because cursive is just
scribbles until third grade.

We live far from anything, a good time is poker and
whiskey in somebody's cabin, but at least I'm working.
This place would blow your mind, so wild civilization
amounts to a dream. Some nights I'd give anything for a
dime to find out if you're still alive and to remind you I'm
your daddy. No matter what goes down, don't let anybody
convince you different. Christ, this is just the start of a
whole lifetime of living apart, and I'm still trying to get it
straight how we're going to manage to stay a family.
McKee brought his kids, but they're boys, and they can
handle the hard hit of British Columbia. My girls would
never get used to peeing outdoors, and the snow keeps it
from being a party. Cash isn't too hot, but I'm trying. I
hated to leave, but it got to where we didn't see each other
that often anyway. Ryan, the bike is still waiting. God

knows I don't have all the answers, maybe I don't have any. Tell your mother things didn't swing the way we planned, but we've still got our daughters, and in the end that'll amount to something. Say a prayer. A kiss to my babies.

Callie tapes the picture of their father above Tessa's crib and every night before they sleep she points to the man with the hooked fish and whispers, It's Dada. Put him in your dreams. Don't forget him, he's your Daddy. He's coming back. You'll see.

TWISTER

All of the grown-ups twisted together become a tangled nest of bodies, and the nest laughs. Callie calls Blue Arm, and they reach for their circles but the bodies collapse. Tessa leaps into the clump of bones and flesh, a pair of legs soars her above the crazy faces.

Give her to me, Callie says, taking Tessa away from the bodies. You'll make her dizzy.

At midnight, 1969 is coming.

In the kitchen, Ryan opens bottles of beer by hooking them under drawer handles and pressing. This trick belongs to Bobby. He said the dents don't matter if you are renting.

On the living room floor, the bodies still webbed, rest. Thighs over elbows, legs braided with legs, toes on necks, heads across stomachs, bouncing up and down, laugh, laugh. Callie says, Come on you guys, let's do it again! But no one is moving.

Their mother looks happy, knotted up with Bobby. Whatever it takes, Bobby jokes, winking at Callie. I told you I'd get her eventually.

I don't know if my kids are ready for this, their mother says.

And Shirl adds, Isn't it time for those kids to be in bed?

But first a kiss, Ray shouts, and the whole party laughs. Come celebrate New Year's Eve with me.

Beer somebody, Shirl calls. And the party repeats, Beer.

In each fist Ryan carries a full beer, in the space between the arms and legs and heads she tiptoes, surrenders the bottles to the first two men that grab.

Come back, come back, Ray cries, clutching Ryan's ankles and trapping her in the human net. It's Twister.

Ryan wrestles against the men that hold her, their strong fingers pinching her skin.

Let go of her! Callie screams. I mean it.

It's just a game, they say, flinging Ryan outside the circle.

But it isn't a game anymore.

GUESTS

Callie wakes to the steel-gray light of a winter morning, snow blowing against her bedroom window, a knock at the door. She steps over the bodies of the sleeping party, opens to more snow on the shoulders of well-dressed strangers. A man and a woman cradling a baby. A small suitcase rests on the floor next to the woman's high-heeled boots.

Happy New Year, the woman says, smiling down on Callie. I'm Abbey. Your mother is expecting me.

The surprise visitors enter without warning, walk into the apartment mess, the tipped beer bottles and the leftover guests. The man shakes his head at the tinseled hats.

Looks like you had quite an evening, he says. Then, to the woman, Abbey, would you mind telling me what we're doing?

Abbey hands him the baby, gently tugs at the tips of her leather gloves. Honey, let's just wait and see. Where's your mother? Abbey asks, her words slow and singsong as if Callie is a young child.

I'll get her, Callie answers. She leaves Abbey and her husband to their gritty whispers, shakes the naked body sprawled under the tangled blanket. Get up, Callie orders. They're inside already.

Into the pillow a hoarse voice pleads, Callie, I have to sleep.

Mother, get up, Callie says, throwing the ratty bathrobe on the bed. Someone named Abbey is standing in our living room.

What? her mother says, bolting up suddenly. Abbey? Oh God, this could only happen to me.

Who is she? Callie asks.

The bathrobe closes on her mother's tired body. My

roommate from St. Mary's. We went to boarding school together. I forgot she was coming. Help me.

Callie runs to the bathroom for cold cream—thick white lotion to wipe away the black mascara smeared over her mother's morning cheeks. A comb too, but she has to hurry.

Everyone's still passed out on the living room floor, Callie says. Abbey doesn't look too happy.

Me either, her mother says, skimming the comb over her snarled hair. This is the best it's going to get.

Then she is out the bedroom door, on her way to greet the waiting family.

Abbey, she says, tightening the rope of her robe. Hello.

Joan, Abbey says in a disgusted tone. This is my husband, Frank. Did you forget we were coming?

Frank's narrowed eyes move slowly over Callie's mother, settle on the chipped paint of her toenails.

Let's sit down, her mother says, ushering them over to the cluttered table. Bowls of stale chips and full ashtrays make Callie sick.

I'd rather stand, Frank says, bouncing the fussy baby. It's all right, honey, he coos. We'll get something to eat soon.

She's tired from the drive, Abbey says. It's a long way from Kansas City.

I suppose, her mother says, reaching for a cigarette.

Abbey's husband clears his throat. The bodies on the floor shift and moan.

What's happening? Ray growls, covers his eyes.

Nothing, her mother says. Go back to sleep. My boss, she tells Abbey.

Shirl's blonde hair falls across Bobby's stomach.

I see, Abbey says. It must have been quite a party.

New Year's Eve, she answers, lifting the sparkling

crown off the table. A tinseled horn falls to the floor. The time just got away from me.

From against the kitchen wall, Callie watches, ashamed of what the outsiders must think.

This is very rude, Frank says, angry. He hands the baby back to Abbey. You two work it out. I'm going to warm up the car and then we're leaving.

Wait, Abbey says. We've been driving all night. Do you have some coffee?

Callie pulls the empty can from the cupboard, opens the lid to display the evidence. Sorry.

Suitcase in hand, he slams the door.

Hey, take it easy, Ray roars.

Callie's mother dumps the garbage of the party into a big brown bag. The Twister dial reminds Callie of the awful last game. Old smoke, beer, the smell of people sleeping in their clothes fill the apartment this morning.

This is no place for a baby, Abbey says, pulling the blanket over the baby's nose. Joan, how could you do this to me? We drove all the way from Kansas City. I thought we could play with our babies, I thought an old friend would be just the thing you need. I had no idea how you were living. You could have told me when I wrote, you could have saved me the trip. Do you realize how embarrassed I am in front of my husband? He'll never forgive me.

I forgot, Callie's mother says, putting the crackers back in the box. I meant to write back. I guess I never thought you were really coming.

What is that supposed to mean? I said I was. She presses the baby into her chest, storms past the sleeping bodies. She stops at the door, her nostrils flaring. Joan, let me tell you, even a bad marriage is better than this.

This is no way to live. Think of your kids. She slams the door behind her.

Who can sleep? Ray says, sitting up. What's the big scene? Didn't you know that broad was coming?

No, her mother says, slumping into his lap, his shoulder a pillow for her drooping head. I can't remember everything.

Don't worry about it, honey, Ray tells her, wrapping her loose hair behind her ear. We're all the friends you'll ever need.

RESCUE

Winter slaps Barren like an angry hand against Callie's cheek. Light ashes of snow blow across the flat fields, while under their feet a crust of ice keeps them from sinking into a cold so deep they could be cast as statues. Walking to school, Ryan and Callie hunch their shoulders in an arc to hold back the shove of a mean freeze. Above them, bare trees beat, stiff limbs coated in icy linen. The earth squeaks under rubber boots. Inside mittens, their fingers curl into tight balls to escape the cold creeping through the loose knit. With each step, Redemption School seems farther away, the winter turning slow minutes into miles.

Out of the woods, Ryan and Callie huddle between houses, the cold has stolen Ryan's voice. Again, Callie tightens the wool scarf over Ryan's mouth, so she can taste her own warm breath. The wet wool is rough on Ryan's tongue. She is too tired to keep trying. The morning ritual repeats itself. Callie tugs down her snowpants, leaving only her uniform skirt to protect against the sting on her knees. Then, the bulky pants are pulled over Ryan's own, two pairs now and her legs can thaw enough to continue the journey. Winter is wicked, but you can't surrender. There are harder things than this ahead.

Ryan, don't start with me, Callie snaps, her voice rushing to the pool in Ryan's eyes. We're almost there. You need to get a thicker skin. I can't take care of you forever.

Windows of warm houses harbor jolly smiles of Styrofoam snowmen, Christmas tree needles litter the edge of the street. Winter is for Christmas, but Christmas is over. This Christmas Eve, Callie left candy canes at every tenant's door. Santa's surprise gifts. But now the neighbors spin out of the apartment parking lot, leaving the girls to make the long walk. The yellow bus of public school kids trudges past, warm faces pressed against the fogged glass. If Callie and Ryan were common, they would be lucky enough to ride, but those schools are for kids who won't ever know God.

At Redemption, cars line the curb, open doors let out heat. Fathers wave good-bye, mothers kiss reluctant lips, eyes in the rear-view mirror check to see their children get inside safely. Sweet morning partings—this is what makes Callie shiver. A lunch box handed over at the last minute, the car disappearing in a cloud of exhaust, and the warm children knowing that, this afternoon, their parents will return for the rescue.

CLEAN

Father Fitzpatrick's housekeeper slices the orange rind in neat sections, four clean knife cuts to prevent the peel from breaking away in bits. They are even lines so your hands stay dry, fingernails saved from the meat that collects underneath. Tongue clicking, Father Fitzpatrick's housekeeper polishes the silver candlesticks, salt and pepper shakers, the tiny crucifix. Her rag wipes away any trace of human prints. On the Oriental tray, there are cubes stacked in a shamrock sugar bowl, a shot glass of whiskey, two rose china cups of Mrs. Needle's tea. Drink, Fitzpatrick says to Ryan, raising the shot glass to his lips. Drink with me.

For Ryan, the first sip of tea begins a bitter brown punishment, the empty cup a relief. In Fitzpatrick's sitting room, the sun delivers delicate lace patterns across the priest's face. Red leather books line the bookcase, there are marble angel's wings and a loose, red ribbon over the black Bible jacket.

Ryan is the only child graced with afternoon teas; she is Fitzpatrick's calling, this gift bestowed because of her sharp memory. Ryan knows the Act of Contrition while the rest of the class is first learning. Performing prayers Fitzpatrick orders her to recite, Ryan earns a chocolate bar and the whole class must clap. On the blackboard, her full name is printed next to the holy reward. Memory is what led Fitzpatrick to tuck her into his pocket, to teach her privately about sacraments and saints.

Some days, she waits in the balcony after school while he arranges his sacristy. Stained glass pictures tell the story of Jesus' suffering, his sunken body collapsing under the weight of the cross. Peter's denial when the rooster crowed. A crown of thorns hooking into Jesus' tender skin.

Ryan feels the horror of nails hammered through his feet. A white kleenex veils Ryan's head. *Oh my God I am heartily sorry*.

Father believes she is blessed. Afternoon teas are a necessity, an hour for training if she is to make her Communion before the rest. A good Irish girl, he tells her. You come from a long line of great martyrs and saints. To understand transubstantiation — he writes the word on a crumpled napkin. You recognize the spelling, yes? — is to understand that miracles are not just fairy tales. God's body actually enters our own. Now isn't that exciting?

Yes, yes, the housekeeper mumbles. Ryan's mouth puckers around the fruit's sour juice. Before Fitzpatrick she had not known about the miracle, Communion was just a flat button of bread you didn't deserve until second grade.

First, you must keep the soul clean, so God enters a tidy home. Can you do that for me?

A black smudge of sin muddies Ryan's soul. Once, Callie hid the Communion host under her tongue and slipped Ryan half in the back pew. God and Fitzpatrick would disapprove. Transubstantiation. But she ate God without knowing. It's too sacred to take, just to see what the wafer tastes like. Maybe she can confess today, in his house, where everything is clean. Or she and Fitzpatrick can trade a sin. A secret she has seen in the cloakroom, while the others went outside to play. Fitzpatrick fumbling to screw the cap back on a bottle of whiskey. To drink in school is wrong, that's why he hides, but still Fitzpatrick eats God's body.

Does sin keep God from entering? Ryan asks.

No, little girl, our souls are all tarnished by sin, but we are made clean by God's good grace.

FORTUNE

Door to door her daughters knock, reading palms for
quarters, trading the future for coins. Bright red scarves
wrap in turbans around their heads and each daughter
wears one of her silver hoop earrings. This collecting of
money embarrasses her. But other kids peddle lemonade,
so she lets them have their day. Callie adds eyeliner and
rouge to the costumes, and they grow into true gypsies;
their long flowered skirts swish across the carpeting.

Their language sounds foreign to her, whispered talk
of love lines, death lines, marriage and divorce. Callie has a
gift for it, she can read past the hand to the heart. But
Callie was born old and dark. She tells the neighbors
things she couldn't know. Here I see you will lose your
first son early, she confides to the woman in 123. Well,
your son has gone to Vietnam, hasn't he?

Lately, the tenants are stopping her daughters in the
parking lot to find out what the next year will bring. They
have magic, the landlord tells her, and she feels forced to
agree. At night, Callie claims to learn wisdom from the
stars; Ryan hears words, too, but she thinks God is talking.

Ray and the guys from the Oasis Tavern throw Shirl a
thirtieth birthday party. Seeking dollars tonight, Callie and
Ryan come in costume, circle the men for money, reach
out for palms to read. Next year you will be married, but
your wife will run away. The one you love loves another.
Beware of pretending. Watch everything. The men laugh,
pay with fives and tens, forget the change. In place of a
present, the girls offer to read Shirl's palm for free. Callie
studies on the right: a long life with much misery. She
points to the fine lines branching out from Shirl's wrist.
Tragedy. And there will be many. Ryan reads her love
lines, three marriages.

The men laugh. Well, you've taken care of the first two.

What about true love? Shirl wants to know. When is that coming?

Callie takes the left palm away from Ryan and stares. One true love but it won't last.

Shirl shouts for good news; the girls insist there isn't any. I read what I read, Callie says.

The men bring Shirl out a giant bottle of bourbon, but Shirl is angry. You kids did this to piss me off.

They're just kids, their mother says. They can't predict anything.

In the morning, while her daughters sleep, she carries their scarves and skirts to the incinerator. The earrings can stay; after all, they belong to her. Their game of fortune falls down with the trash of the Barren Apartments and vanishes quickly into fire and smoke. This afternoon she will sign them up for piano, ballet, or flute, and the future will be what it has to be, a mystery.

Finished

PIANO

Callie's mother says even poor girls should play piano. Poise, she calls it, while the moving men hunch under the burden of the white upright. You can thank Ray, she says. He got it at a good price.

The keys are gray and dirty, some of them silent while others stick. Callie likes the black keys best. Sharp and flat. At school she begins lessons.

Keep practicing, Sister Anne Eugene says, the metronome a strict tick. *Three blind mice, Three blind mice.* Sister clips Callie's nails. No clicking on the keys. Listen, girlie, this is simple hygiene. Outside the music room window, the fifth grade girls chase the boys, steal their hats in a wild game of Pom-Pom Pullaway. Eyes on the music, Sister taps her pointer against the sheet. Concentrate, girlie.

After school, Ryan makes up words for songs and they perform shows for Tessa. Tessa learns to clap and dance. Noise, their mother says at night, closing the cover over the dingy keys. I can't come home after working all day and listen to that pounding.

Ryan writes a song for the scales, *All Bad Children Don't Easily Forget God*, and Callie plays it on black notes only. Sister's face is disapproving. That isn't music, Sister says. Play like a nice girl should. White key melodies of nursery rhymes and lullabies.

Nice girls don't interest Callie. I want to play like the radio, rock and roll.

Those songs are for sinners. Piano is a way to pray. Sister closes her eyes to demonstrate, every note slow and holy, like a choir in a church balcony. Learn to give glory. God is listening. A girl from your background can't afford to indulge in rock and roll. I'm sure it wouldn't take much to push you off a cliff. Piano will give you purity.

Poise and purity. Callie tells her mother she's quitting, and her mother says, Yes, please. Poor girls don't need poise, they need money.

FLYING

Darlene's fingertips smooth soft circles into Callie's temples. This is the only spot that can take you under, Darlene says.

Behind Callie's eyes, yellow flames of candles scatter. On the floor next to Callie, Ryan lies stretched out, practicing her turn for the trance, a chance to enter the other world.

Darlene has promised to link their spirits with their father. Your eyelids are getting heavier and heavier, Darlene whispers, her words creeping slow and deep like sleep. You are dropping through a long tunnel, your body floats without gravity.

Goosebumps prickle Callie's flesh, she falls easily, her bones sinking beneath the carpeting, through the cool dirt of earth.

You are light as a feather, Darlene's voice spirals with the rubbing.

Everywhere there is space and the gentle touch of air against skin. Callie's clothes melt away.

Now you are climbing a staircase of clouds, you rise without weight.

Fluttering heart soars toward the ceiling. Callie's soul has left her body.

You are in the sky now; decide where you want to fly and begin the journey.

Blue sea of heaven surrounds Callie; British Columbia waits minutes away. Her soul is carried by the warm light of sunshine.

Look down, Darlene whispers. Don't be afraid.

Trees. The pointed tips of evergreens. Roads twisting through a mountain village. Snow. A thick forest buries her father. Where will she find him? Will the boy be there? Dad, Callie cries, her voice echoing. It's me, Callie.

In the sky Callie hangs, wanting to believe.

Trust in your connection, Darlene says.

Callie stays hovering, afraid the fall through the trees will kill her instantly. Dad, it's me.

He hears, Darlene says. Wait for him to appear.

Suddenly, he is there, face without body, face larger than Callie's. What is it, sweet baby?

Yes, it is him exactly. The trance works magic. Can you come back?

Honey, he says smiling, your daddy is busy. What is it you need?

We need you in Barren.

Soon, he says, and his face fades into ripples of water.

Wait! I believe. I believe! Come back to me.

But now there is only a suitcase flying past, inside it his clothes piled in a loose heap. Her hands reach, touch nothing. He has disappeared completely.

Callie's spirit sinks, crashes against the carpeting. There is the scratch of wool against her skin, hot wax burns the scent of cherries.

Blink and you are back, Darlene says.

Eyes open, Callie returns to the white walls, nearly grey, the dirt-filmed windows of their basement apartment. It is the same. Ryan sleeps, her mouth open, breath lazy. She has missed everything.

Did you see him? Darlene asks, her sharp fingernails tickling Callie's temples.

Darlene, Callie says, the skin of her neck tingling. Even if souls can travel, what difference does it make?

It makes a difference, Darlene says. But you have to have faith.

VICTORY

Callie slides the sliver of paper into the thin slit of Earl's mailbox. The coded note reads: SWEETTARTS UNDER THE WILLOW TREE. Callie takes Ryan into her game, a secret too good to keep. And Earl hangs on, such an easy player. Callie orders and he obeys. Since the car ride, she has been forbidden to see him, but the game is a way to get the goods without punishment. This Easter vacation the girls are free to leave notes every day, tiny requests for gifts Earl always honors, gifts dropped off in the willow's secret cranny. No one has caught them yet, but they imagine the danger, relish the risk.

Earl has plenty of money, Callie tells Ryan. Don't worry about that. Besides, he's lonely. This game gives him something to do.

Earl makes the drop late afternoon before he heads off for his job at the radio station. Callie and Ryan spy from the window of their apartment, giggle at Earl's gangling walk toward the willow. They know his pockets carry candy, sweets they will eat after Earl's car disappears down the street. Earl bends down, tucks the payment into the tiny hollow, then turns to be sure no one is watching.

Tomorrow a new note will make bigger demands. They have decided to see how far Earl will go to keep playing. That's part of the game, pushing Earl to quit.

He can't say no to me, Callie says. She does not care about the gifts; it is the rush of power that thrills her, Earl's willing surrender. An eager prisoner, he plays the game to come clean with Callie. And, after the drive, Callie is anxious to see Earl pay for his mistake. The purple fur of his front seat has turned Callie against the color. She hates it the way she hates the ugly bulge of Earl's huge Adam's apple.

Tomorrow's note will request a record for their own phonograph, a top ten single, a hit he will hate to part with. They listen to the loud roar of Earl's motor grow smaller as he moves toward the highway. Then the girls are out of the building, stretched out on the cool dirt, watching the world from behind the swaying curtain of the willow. Sweettarts fizz on their tongues, their teeth crush the tart candy in mouth-watering celebration, sour taste of victory.

THE FLOOD

Snow melts so fast the Minnesota River swells and spills its heavy load down the roads of Barren. Even the bridge out of town is closed. Barren is a swamp of wet land. The girls join the other kids taking off their clothes, wade down the creek of streets. Spring has returned, the sky opens its wide heart to the world, birds sing to welcome in the warmth. Salamanders wiggle their spotted bodies past the window of their basement apartment. Callie and Ryan catch one for a pet. But inside, its skin turns dry and thin; they fill the bathtub to offer it a new home.

This is one pet you can't keep, their mother screams. The salamander dog paddles back down the muddy street.

It has been a long silence between letters, but Callie can't let go of him. There are stories about Barren she has saved, and when British Columbia ends, he will hold her close while she tells him the worst of it. Her tape recorder collects tales of these days, long talks Callie whispers under the blankets while the rest of her family sleeps. It is important he hear the scary parts. She makes her voice shake, urgent and afraid. It is a father's job to keep his family safe. Under her bed, the reels of tape wait in a cigar box. If her mother finds them first, Callie's truth will mean trouble.

Tomorrow, she tells him, is Easter. This year there are no nice dresses or gloves for Sunday Mass. She is sorry she cannot look her best. Church will be horrible, the other families will stare. He always wanted her to be a real beauty. But there is little you can do without money. Still, she has become a good father. And today, she sloshed down the wet roads to downtown Barren for plastic eggs filled with small toys and candy so Ryan can still believe. It is too early for Tessa to understand the bunny or the reason for the holiday, but the egg will make her happy. Baskets would be better, but there is no money. Now that her sisters are asleep, she will creep into the living room and make magic happen.

Easter is a day to celebrate being saved, she tells him, a sign that suffering is past. The sacrifice of Lent ends and candy can come back. Father Fitzpatrick said even the flood was God's sign of a new beginning. The water washes away the sins of Barren. It's spring, a time to start over, she whispers into the microphone. You can come home this summer, and we'll begin again. This time, a good family.

M.I.A.

Evelyn's father flounders in the thick weeds of the Vietnam jungle. His plane shot from the sky, he wanders through swamps and tall reeds, fighting his way back to Barren. Now there are no more letters for Evelyn, either. News of the crash buzzes through the building, sentences passed ear to ear like a telephone game played at birthday parties. Bobby goes upstairs to Evelyn's apartment to talk to her mother; there are things he knows from being there, things he must tell her. They talk through the space of the chained door.

M.I.A., Bobby says when he comes down. Taken prisoner maybe, but the plane is still missing.

What does it mean? Callie asks Bobby. Does it mean he won't be back?

Who knows, Bobby answers, his eyes closed. It could mean anything.

Missing In Action. Callie knows. A man tries to return to his daughter, but the enemy sucks him under, shackles his ankles, locks him in a cell. Fathers disappear every day, she wants to tell Bobby, but you have to keep hoping. It is the wait, like time exploding, that brings the worst pain.

It could have been me, it could have been anybody, Bobby says, lifting the four dog tags to his lips. The medals jingle like tiny bells.

In the field, Ryan and Callie collect daisies to take to Evelyn as an offering, small flowers with new white petals to say they are sorry.

Evelyn never even comes out to play, Ryan says. What will we say when they answer the door?

All winter Evelyn's mother has kept her inside their tidy apartment. When the girls pass them in the hallway, Evelyn presses her face against her mother's leg. Callie has told Ryan that Evelyn's mother is wicked, a woman who believes she's above the rest, but today they must forgive her. There is a bigger war at stake.

We'll just say we're praying for his safety.

Callie and Ryan wrap a jelly jar in tissue paper. New buds will open in a few days, and the flowers will remind Evelyn and her mother that others have joined in their wait. Callie knocks, Ryan stands behind her, afraid. Chain on the door, Evelyn's mother glares down on the girls.

What do you want from me? Evelyn's dull head peeks out from behind her mother's hip.

We heard about your husband, Callie says, holding out the gift of flowers.

Heard from who? the voice bites back.

Bobby said he was Missing In Action.

Bad news certainly travels fast.

We brought you flowers to say we're sorry.

Evelyn's mother sneers at the homemade vase. Thank you anyway, but Evelyn has allergies. No doubt those flowers would make her sneeze. Why don't you give them to your mother? I'm sure she would be impressed with your ingenuity.

No, Callie says, holding them forward. They're for you. At least keep the vase.

Little homemade trifles won't return my husband, Evelyn's mother's voice crackles.

He's coming home, Callie says. We're praying.

That's wonderful, Evelyn's mother snaps. Prayer hasn't brought your father back, has it?

No, but he's coming.

You girls have enough drama of your own. I don't think you need to go digging where you don't belong. It's unkind to revel in other people's tragedies.

Evelyn's mother closes the door on the daisies. Her big

words are a puzzle, but Callie sees the picture. She knocks again; she must explain.

Go away, Evelyn's mother hisses. Go play in the highway.

You were right, Ryan says. She's wicked.

Yes, Callie says. Wicked and afraid.

MARTYRS AND SAINTS

Ryan understands the story of Our Lady of Fatima and
feels sorry the children were misunderstood. But
everything for God means suffering. Even if you are bad in
the beginning, you can win God back by dying. Ryan
understands the children's vision because she has seen
Mary, many times, at her prayer rock in the woods.

Mary comes to her when Ryan closes her eyes very
tightly and prays with her whole soul. *Virgin Mary I do
believe.* At school, the sixth grade girls were reciting this in
the bathroom, holding hands around the toilet, chanting,
waiting for Mary's face to form in the water. Father Fitzpatrick said a lavatory wasn't fit for the Blessed Mother to
appear, so the ceremony stopped.

But at the prayer rock, the world is solemn and holy,
and Ryan rubs the plastic cover of her scapular until Mary
finally comes to her. At the feet of the flowing blue gown,
Ryan leaves tokens for offerings: lilacs, holy cards, a glow-
in-the-dark rosary. Mary's kind hands bless Ryan's head,
but she gives no message, no words to spread that will
redeem all sinners. Ryan knows that when her spirit is
completely pure, Mary will send her on a mission, but
maybe that will take years. There is nothing more beautiful
than being a martyr, giving your life as a gift to God. This
is what Mary has taught her—keep believing and someday
God will lift you up. Even Mary was surprised when the
angel came for her. Maybe no one ever knows for sure if
they're good enough.

The prayer rock must remain a secret, even from
Callie, who thinks Ryan makes things up. Later, when

Mary is ready, Callie can help the miracle happen. Then, everyone in Barren will praise the girls for their sacred vision. A white light heats Ryan's heart. Someday soon, her turn is coming.

FINISHED

Her divorce decree appears in the newspaper. Shirl clips the thin line of print with a manicure scissors and tapes it to the refrigerator. It's finished, Shirl says. You're famous. Famous and free. Now you can marry a doctor and get in on the cash. I, for one, am tired of working for a living.

Neither of them have ever met an available doctor in Barren, but truth doesn't cloud Shirl's dreams.

Don't let the girls see that, she says, raising her eyebrows at her vital statistic. They're not ready.

They'll be grateful someday, Shirl says, plopping her bathrobed body on the sofa. Believe me. On the coaster Shirl's Diet-Rite sweats. Shirl is one for easy mornings. Throw me a smoke, will you, honey? Shirl inhales deep, opens her mouth like a wide door, lets the smoke find its own way out.

There are things about kids Shirl will never understand. A dad's a dad, she tells Shirl. And this one's Christ reincarnated.

You could set them straight, Shirl says, sliding her big toe over the bulging bunions of the other foot. I got to quit working on my feet. The important thing here is — you're free to remarry.

Shirl's ex-husbands are both characters from a bad act, and she's only thirty.

Shirl, you can't do that with daughters. They'd never let a string of men in. They only want their real father.

Well, they don't know what they're missing. My motto is: The more the merrier. They'll give up on him eventually. He hasn't written much, has he?

Not much.

At first his silence was a great gift, but now Callie's

daily trips to the mailbox make her wish he would write. His absence keeps him floating over their apartment like an angel of mercy, his spirit canonized during Callie's bedtime stories. Her girls are caught in the glossy web of memory, and she can't trade them facts for fantasy.

We already know what you think, Callie hisses, whenever she tries to kick the pedestal out from under him. Keep your opinions to yourself, please.

Callie could get her face slapped good for sass, but why bother. Callie reigns as queen. Already she has turned Ryan against her, pretending to be the better mother. At least Tessa will belong to her someday.

It's a hard thing to raise kids only to lose them to a missing father, she tells Shirl. But Shirl isn't listening; she is carried away in a romance magazine. Well, they'll know when they have their own kids. And what does the chintzy settlement prove? Nothing. Ten dollars a week. If he cares so much, where's the money? Even a no-show at his own hearing. Let them try to collect while he's in Canada.

What do you do with *our* checks? Callie wants to see the bills, spitting out *our* like it was her money. Groceries and rent are boring. He would buy them candy, new clothes, maybe even that horse Callie wants so badly. There are no checks lately, but Callie thinks she's lying. This from her first baby, the one she carried, her bare feet cold on the wooden floor. Night after night waiting for him to come home once the bars closed, but he didn't. It was the weight of Callie's small body in her arms that made her want a real family. Babies have a way of making a heart hope for a life that isn't coming.

Get looking for Mr. Right, Shirl says, propping the open magazine against her large breasts.

Shirl, she says. There are no saviors.

Take my advice. Your face won't hold out forever. Get going now before it's too late.

It's finished, but not really. Too late was when she married him.

Mercy

WHAT'S LEFT

Shirl's apartment is wet ash and a burnt spring where her bed used to be. A cigarette got away in her sleep. Her knees bent into her chest, Shirl sits on the kitchen floor, yellowed hands trembling. I need a Bloody Mary.

Shirl and their mother rest their heads together, twirl sticks of soft celery in slow motion.

Callie says, It could have been us.

Shut up, her mother answers back.

Ryan sees Chimp and Teddy sizzling in a blaze of loose stuffing.

Barren could kill anybody, almost killed me, Shirl says, mascara smears on her cheeks. Her brother owns a trailer court in Tennessee, not too far from Elvis Presley. In Tennessee, Shirl will get a fresh start.

I wish I was leaving, their mother says, fingering back the edges of Shirl's singed hair. Please don't move. You can live with us till you're back on your feet.

But no smoking, Callie says, afraid of Shirl falling asleep.

My kids think they're the goddamn police, their mother says. It drives me crazy.

No, Shirl says, nothing can keep me. Not a house, not money, not even a good man. Of course there isn't a good man in Barren.

Callie offers Shirl some of the money she's been saving, and Shirl accepts. As soon as I'm settled, you'll hear from me. You girls be good to your mother, she needs all the help she can get.

From the basement window, they wave and watch the cab take Shirl away.

It's always the same, their mother says.

After Shirl's fire, their mother comes home from work

every night, makes dinner, reads Tessa to sleep, and cleans the apartment on Saturday mornings. Callie shows her mother how to make beds the way Darlene taught them, and Ryan learns how to polish a mirror without leaving streaks. The girls wait for Shirl's postcard, but their mother says it's never coming. People forget, she says. Forgetting is easy.

CONFIRMATION

Confirmation has come at last. For months, Callie and her class have prepared for this day, the sacrament where the Holy Spirit enters your body and you take a new name. She will be called Joan, after her mother and the brave French woman who led the battles.

At school they studied their names and the saints' stories. Sister gave a little party each day to honor a different name. On her day, Callie traced a picture from her *Sixty Saints For Girls*, and colored it in perfectly. St. Joan's sword stood for courage, and the crown on her head meant glory. She told the whole class tales of St. Joan's struggle, and afterward Father came in to give her name a blessing. In front of the class, he laid his hands on Callie's shoulders and prayed. *Alleluia, alleluia. You have played a man's part and kept your courage high. The Lord gave you firmness of resolve and your name shall be ever blessed, alleluia.* And the whole class answered, *Pray for us St. Joan, holy woman that you are, and the Lord's true worshipper, alleluia.* When the prayer was over, Father hung a medal of St. Joan around Callie's neck, and today she wears it safe against her chest, like Bobby wears his dog tags.

Her mother pulls the spongy pink rollers from Callie's hair, twists the ringlets around her fingers, combs them into elegant curls. Then, she ties back Callie's hair with a white ribbon. A perfect bow, like an angel's wings, rests on top of Callie's ponytail. Ryan and Tessa are ready, dressed in their best clothes, and now it is time to pull the new, white dress over Callie's head, carefully, to keep her hair neat.

Let me do it, her mother says, lowering the scratchy, starched fabric over Callie's shoulders.

Pretty, Tessa says.

The dress has come from the city, a dress her mother chose, and Callie loves it, the high lace neck, the ruffled cuffs. Her mother buttons the back.

You look terrific, she says. But then you should; that dress cost more than I make in one day.

Ryan holds out the shiny white shoes. Are you ready? she asks, setting them at Callie's feet. The lace tights slide easy against the leather.

This is your day, honey, her mother says.

Confirmation is all that Callie has hoped for. Except that her father will not be here to see her kneeling in front of the full church, her head bent over the altar rail in prayer, the archbishop's hands on her beautiful head. He could not make it home, he wrote. But on her day she will be in his prayers. Tonight she will get out her tape recorder and tell him everything, how her picture of St. Joan won the coloring contest, about the reception with cake and punch in the church basement, her dress, the best one in the class. She will tell how the Holy Spirit's flame filled her soul with fire, as it did the apostles'.

Callie takes the gloves away from Tessa. You can play with them later. Okay? Then she bends over, offers Tessa her cheek. Give Callie a kiss. You be a good baby today, do it for Callie.

Wash your hands before you put those on, her mother says. You want them to be clean.

Finally, Callie is ready. In the mirror she admires her face, the lace collar of her new dress frames it perfectly. A crown would be wonderful, but crowns are reserved for saints and queens.

Well, her mother says, her reflection smiling out at Callie. I'm proud of you. I guess you've grown into a real lady.

Yes, Callie says. And a brave one, too.

TOWERS

Across the Barren Highway silos break the sky like magical towers in a mystical kingdom. Clyde and Jerry have made the journey there, have told the girls of a path to the river where barges come to fill their bellies with grain, and of an empty boxcar covered with names. The boys want to show them the way, but Callie says no. She and Ryan will try it alone. They pack Ryan's bookbag with Clyde's gifts: a pencilled map, two cigarettes and a can of red spray paint. The girls are ready.

Along the ditch, they kick the rubber toes of their tennis shoes against broken beer bottles, rusted cans. Cars on the highway whoosh past.

Take my hand, Callie tells Ryan. We have to be careful crossing.

On the other side, railroad tracks stretch into a long road of identical slats disappearing into deep grass. The boxcar, painted with words and hearts and crosses, waits to join a moving train: *Billy loves Cindy, Clyde and Jerry, Class of '68.*

This is it, Callie says, dropping the bag, reaching inside for their can of paint. What should we say?

Ryan would like to write a long story, but the red sprays on in huge blotches, making the letters fat and messy.

Let's just do our names.

Callie goes first, aims high, presses her finger hard on the tiny white nozzle. Fine lines of red run down the curve of her *C.*

Save some for me, Ryan says, afraid her chance is never coming.

Don't worry, Callie says. There's plenty. Callie writes her name next to *Clyde* and *Jerry.*

Clyde will like that, she tells Ryan. He has a crush on me.

Everyone has a crush on you, Ryan tells Callie.

Finished finally, she hands the can to Ryan. Shake it first, she says. In Ryan's hand, tiny beads rattle against the inside of the can.

She spells her name, larger than Callie's.

Keep going, Callie says. See if you can get through Barren. Write small so it lasts.

The tiny eye of the little *e* fills with paint. It looks like a *c*, Ryan tells Callie.

Don't worry, Callie says. They'll know what you mean. She takes the can back. Adds *1969* underneath *Barren*. The can hisses, then sputters, empty.

Ryan walks backward into the weeds to get the big picture. Soon the boxcar will chug through stations where children gather along the tracks to wave at the engineer. The children will see their names, imagine their story. *Callie* and *Ryan* will ride through strange cities like an important message.

Callie heaves her body up into the open doorway.

Come on, she tells Ryan, let's look inside. She bends over, offers Ryan a hand, pulls her in by the belt loop of her blue jeans.

Inside there is darkness and the sour smell of wet hay.

This would make a great hideaway, Ryan says, remembering the story of *The Boxcar Children*, a family of orphans who made their home in an abandoned boxcar. Let's come back with Clyde and Jerry, have a picnic.

Look at this, Callie says, lifting an army blanket. I bet somebody sleeps here. In the corner, she finds an empty wine bottle and a beat-up umbrella. Sitting in the open doorway, they dangle their legs over the track, twirl them in circles, wrap them together like pretzels. The May sun beats through their jeans, heats their legs. They stare at the silos, the towers that seem to begin at the top of the trees. Ryan would like to climb one, to see Barren as a tiny town, the way a bird must. In stories, the towers are places to watch the enemy, or a prison to protect a beautiful young princess. Sometimes on the playground swingset, Ryan pretends she can fly, and her toes point toward the sky, trying to reach the world of the silos.

Let's get going, she tells Callie, as Callie falls back on the hay. Straw sticks to the black strands of Callie's hair.

What for? she says. We're in no hurry.

Let's save the cigarettes for the river, Ryan says, anxious to lie on the steep bank, take in the sight of the barges' slow travel.

Okay, Callie says.

Callie props her hands behind her head, hooks her ankles together, sighs a heavy breath. It's been almost a year, she says.

What does that mean? Ryan asks.

It means we actually live here, Callie says, pronouncing *here* like a disgusting word. It means we're here permanently.

Maybe we'll move when Dad comes back, Ryan says. She knows Callie's dream, and the hope that keeps Callie going.

Maybe, Callie says. We'll see.

Do you think Dad will see our names in British Columbia? Ryan asks.

No, Callie says. For all we know, this boxcar is never leaving.

Ryan hears a branch crack, rustle of something moving in the weeds. Listen, she whispers, tapping the sole of Callie's shoe. Something's coming.

Clyde and Jerry, Callie says.

But Ryan sees the whiskered face and the heavy brown overcoat. The man drags one leg.

Callie, Ryan says, get up.

What are you doing here? he growls. This is certified federal property. Trespassing.

He grabs Ryan's leg, pulls her to the ground; the sharp stones of the track cut through the knee of her jeans.

Hey, Callie says, sitting up suddenly. What do you think you're doing?

She must be punished, the man says, his hands tight around Ryan's wrist. The crime is not a misdemeanor.

Let her go, Callie says, jumping down. She hasn't done anything.

Does God pervert judgment and does the Almighty distort justice? the man says. She has written the message. He shakes Ryan's wrist, stares at the paint-stained tips of her fingers. On the boxcar, their names shine wet in the sun.

That's not us, Callie says.

Liars, the man says. The wicked shall perish. I know who you are. His words expose cracked teeth, the thick meat of his tongue.

Callie grabs the sleeve of his coat. His arm swings back, a slap against Callie's cheek.

Go, she screams. Ryan races, Callie's feet beat the ground behind her.

Hang on to me, Callie says, catching up. Don't stop till I say so.

The girls scramble across the highway, dodging traffic, run past the Barren Dairy, pull open the heavy door of the apartment building. They tumble down the stairs in one large step. Callie slams the door, turns the lock, pulls the chain. She drops to the floor, struggles to catch her breath.

My bookbag, Ryan says.

Forget it, Callie says. We can't go back.

Ryan runs to the back window, looks out toward the highway. She will never cross over to that other world, never go back for her bookbag, never follow that path to the river. In the stories, the towers have guards, but they are good soldiers with tall blue hats strapped on under their chins. Handsome men. But Barren is not a kingdom, and the silos aren't towers, just places to store grain. Ryan touches the rip in her jeans. Warm blood trickles from the cut in her knee.

He doesn't know where we live, Callie says, joining Ryan at the window. We're safe.

No, Ryan says. Not now. He knows our names.

DREAMS

Craig's number is up. Darlene's boyfriend is going.
The girls will get a new sitter and Darlene will wait in
Wisconsin until boot camp ends. Then they'll get married.
Darlene runs blue lipstick over her thick lips and dabs after
with a kleenex. She has loved blue since she saw Lulu in
To Sir With Love. On the bed the girls gather around her
and beg her to stay with them while Craig serves his
country. She still has her job at the truck stop. Darlene is
the best sitter; she tells true stories of murders she reads
about in confession magazines, her voice haunting when it
comes to the actual killing. She makes the girls terrified to
sleep.

But today she tells about a farmhouse in Dearling,
down the road from her folks, with a garden full of
vegetables: cucumbers, beans, tomatoes. Apple trees.
Daffodils in the spring. In Dearling, you can live happy till
the day you die. She says Barren brought her love and
now love calls her to another place. When love whistles
you walk, or you end up alone.

Darlene's boyfriend, Craig, is glad to quit trucking.
After his training in the war, it will be easier to be
somebody. His kisses remind Darlene of Steve McQueen.
Imagine Craig with a shaved head, she says, flopping
backwards on the bed, giggling. Darlene sings *The Ballad of
the Green Beret*, her voice sweet and jazzy. Craig will wear
his uniform, crisp green for the groom. No medals yet, but
he will still look snazzy. Her dress will be a white satin
strapless with an elegant trail and a deep V dipping between her full breasts. Sexy, so that Craig will remember
what he's missing. Close your eyes, she tells the girls. Picture my wedding.

Ryan knows the exact dress that Darlene means. It was Barbie's dress when Barbie and Ken got married.

I picture a dress just like Barbie's, Ryan says.

Yes, Darlene says, closing her arms across herself. Like Barbie's, only better.

THE BLESSING

Father Fitzpatrick finishes his second shot of whiskey and begins the blessing. *Almighty God we humbly beseech Thee to bless and sanctify this house.* His holy water rains over the ragged plaid couch, the ring-stained coffee table, the broken xylophone in pieces on the floor, and the ancient upright piano. It falls like good weather on the green shag carpeting. *And all who dwell within and everything else in it.* Ryan has brought him home for an apartment blessing.

Her daughters' eyelids are clenched like fists, the rapture of children trusting a magician. Their fingers reach up into holy steeples. *Grant to them the abundance of heavenly blessings. And finally, direct their desires to the fruits of Thy mercy.* Tessa squirms in Callie's lap. Pressed in prayer, her tiny hands are trapped between Callie's. Sometimes she opens her eyes for a peek, but Callie and Ryan have floated far away, have sailed off on the sea of Fitzpatrick's wavy chanting.

This passion for God was their father's doing, he pushed for baptisms and Sunday Mass. And where was he now? In another country, showing up in a couple of letters, no cash.

May the angels of Thy light dwell within the walls of this house. May the angels protect it and give the strength of stones to the spirits of those who dwell within. Through Christ Our Lord Amen, Fitzpatrick says. And her girls are giddy as a birthday party.

Can he stay for supper?

Yes, my lovelies, Fitzpatrick says. But first, another drink.

In slurred handwriting, he scrawls their name and address under a full-color picture of Jesus. A horrible picture

Ryan will insist on hanging. His heart, raw, red flesh, and a golden flame rising from it.

Father, she asks, is that burning heart necessary?

Of course, my dear. For suffering. For grace.

Her girls each claim a knee.

Callie lifts Tessa up. Father, she says, I'm already teaching her *Now I Lay Me Down to Sleep*.

Wonderful, Fitzpatrick says. Perhaps your dear mother would allow me another taste of that whiskey?

She reaches for the shotglass.

Oh, my dear, he says, holding out his glass. Don't bother measuring.

Fitzpatrick shakes, the whiskey drips on Tessa's leg.

Father, Ryan says, does this mean God will be with us always?

Always, he says, kissing their foreheads. God will take care of you, my beautiful babies.

Tomorrow she will tack up the picture, let the heart burn over their days. They can have their blessing. Why should she take it away? After all, what is faith but a last hope that somewhere, someone kind is listening?

Sheila O'Connor was born and raised in Minneapolis, Minnesota, where she currently lives with her husband and daughter. She received a Master of Fine Arts degree from the University of Iowa. A recipient of a Loft-McKnight Fellowship, her poems and stories have appeared in a number of literary magazines, including *Helicon Nine*, *Sing Heavenly Muse*, and *Three Rivers Poetry Journal*. She teaches writing classes through The Loft, COMPAS Writers-in-the-Schools program, The Minnesota State Arts Board, and other organizations.